Dark Secrets

Elaine M. Aitken

GW00500087

ISBN 9781521215975

Acknowledgements

Many friends and family have helped and encouraged me during the writing of this book but as usual there are a few to whom I owe special thanks and without whom the book would not have been published.

Chrissie Middleton and Mandy O'Connor, read the story as I wrote it, keeping me on my toes by asking when the next chapter would be ready. Thanks also to the lovely ladies at my writing groups who listened to the book week after week and added their suggestions and comments, and to Brigitte Clarkson, who checked the French bits for me, and my brother-in-law John King for his ideas and assistance.

A big thank you to brilliant fellow writer David Antocci in the US for his encouragement, and also Scott Gaunt for his excellent graphic design work for the cover.

Last, but most important of all, my proof reader, editor in chief, text formatter, head cook and tea maker and general Man Friday for everything technical, my amazing husband, Douglas.

I raise my glass to you all.

Contents

Introduction

Dark Secrets is an adventure set 250 years in the future, in the summer of 2265. The story begins on the starship USS Temeraire where hideous secrets are concealed. The atmosphere aboard is very surreal with some passengers disappearing, and others behaving strangely.

With Andrew's persistence and Jay's unique ability, they discover the truth about what is happening on the ship. What they find out is so terrifying they decide to abandon everything they have ever known. They become part of a small group of conspirators, whose aim is to publicly denounce the actions of the Universal Peace Guardians towards the citizens of Newton-Aldrin on Mars.

Jay and Andrew know they can never return home and have to adjust to living on Earth forever in order to achieve their goal.

1

Daring to explore

Rules are made to be broken, so when Andrew suggested exploring this inter-galactic space ship I jumped at the chance. Unfortunately we were caught by a robot and had to make a run for it.

I'd better start from the beginning otherwise I shall confuse myself and get into a muddle.

It has been two days since we left Mars. I think this is some kind of hospital ship. We have met no grown-ups but I know several came aboard with us. We have controlled freedom of the ship, not that this is much, only one level and only part of that. We are banned from the other levels and cargo areas. The robotic crew keep tabs on us.

There are seven of us, teenagers that is, who came aboard together for this special trip to Earth. I assume we all need to have surgery that can't be carried out at home, because that's why I'm here. There's a boy who can't walk, he's in a wheelchair, and twins who are blind. Another boy walks awkwardly with two sticks and there's a red haired girl who can't use her right arm and hand. The other is just, well, weird! Perhaps he suffers from some form of Autism, although it can't be that bad as he joined in with some of the games. There is another group but they were here before us and apart from being a bit dreary and dull, seem very ordinary, you know, no obvious problems or disabilities.

I spend most of my time gazing out at the universe or reading, having not much contact with anybody unless I have to. I'm amazed by the splashes of colour that appear in space. I know some people see colour when they listen to music but for me it is the other way round; I see colour and it forms music in my head. If I'm quick enough I can write it down, but that's not easy. You see, if you are a writer your thoughts can be spoken aloud and automatically transferred into text. Music must be hand written on staves and takes forever. I tried humming into a recording device, which works to an extent, but, as my hearing deteriorates someone will have to help me transcribe it.

It's really frustrating. As colours change, music fills my brain, sometimes it's almost painful and I feel trapped inside my head. What I need is a programme that will directly transcribe what I hear into written music. A communications link plugged through my ear to my brain would be good! Dream on, pal.

My parents found out I was different when I was fifteen months old. They had taken me to a Holographic Firework display. I now know that I screamed afterwards for three hours! They assumed I didn't like fireworks and it was a couple of days later that my mother handed me my first book, a bright blue book, and I told her it made a very loud noise!

Things gradually made sense to her – my only wanting white toys in my cot. I should explain that white noise is to me a fuzzy distant tone. When it is on its own, I've learned to ignore it; perhaps it's akin to tinnitus, I'm not sure. Bright colours trigger a symphony of melody depending how they form and

2

follow each other. I can now appreciate and actually enjoy fireworks, but I have to be on my own.

You're probably wondering how I can manage to live a normal life at all, and I don't know if I could anywhere else but Mars. You see Newton-Aldrin is a very dull city. Because everything has to be transported from Earth, buildings are all the same, made from preformed sections, some as long as fifty metres. The city is merging shades of greyish beige.

Quarters are stacked in blocks to use the area most efficiently and there is no individuality. Your home is the same as everyone else's; furniture, blinds, bedding, all identical. My brain can cope with the dull beige of outpost life. I have special glasses which cut out colour in books and things. I don't know how they work, but they do, otherwise I could not have gone to school.

Everyone wears the same white clothing, even babies. When they outgrow anything it is sent back to Clothing Base for a larger size. Nothing ever seems to wear out and be thrown away.

Looking back to when we left Mars, I had never seen such views before. You can see the colour which is why it's known as the Red planet. You never see any of the local terrain when you live there, as life is spent within the climate controlled city of Newton-Aldrin. A city of about a hundred thousand inhabitants and so named, in some perverse way, because of the anti-gravity propulsion needed for inter-galactic travel and the second man to walk on Earth's moon nearly three hundred years ago. (The original settlement on the Moon was named after Armstrong, the first man to set foot there.)

This is an old transport class ship, at least thirty

years old, and has none of the more sophisticated modern inventions on board for us kids to play with. Any younger ones would be tucked away in the nursery or the school rooms but we teenagers lazed in bed for the first two mornings playing games in the lounge later. There are several old gaming machines, but then someone found a copy of an ancient game in a cupboard. It's called "Monopoly" and now there is always a rush to join in. It seems to be some sort of property game, where you buy bits of cities and houses and things. But, as no-one owns anything on Mars, I can't see the point.

Uh oh! There goes the buzzer. Time for the next pill, bor-ing! Did I say that we don't eat actual food? Nothing like the things my great-great-great-grandparents would have eaten on Earth. I have seen a picture of them sitting around a big table. Mum says this is her family and points to her great-great-great-grandmother in a baby seat. But she's not sure who the other people are. She and Dad are both third generation Mars. Sound explodes as I look at the bright clothes and food in the photograph. I can't imagine eating anything green or orange! What looks like a tree stands in the corner of the room. It's decorated with bright coloured shiny balls. On the back of the photo it says 'Winter Thanksgiving Festival, December 2123.'

Because of the transportation issues we eat only pills. When the planet was first colonised it was hoped that it would be self-sufficient in food production. We learned about the various experiments they did, but the fine balance of everything needed to form a stabilised world just wouldn't work. Too boring to go into all the details but we do have our own gas conversion units, to keep the atmosphere as it should be, and, of course, there is the refinery for water. I don't like to think too much about the recycling of water, sufficient to say that it is, all of it. But the glass we get to drink with our pills tastes OK. The arboretum is a hangover from those early experimental days. Some of the trees are over two hundred years old. I have been there and seen them and the flowers, but I can't stay long, too noisy. I wonder what Earth will be like. There'll be so much colour everywhere, will my brain explode?

It is now two days later and I've made friends with Andrew. He's the one who I thought may be autistic, but he's not. He's a genius! The others threw him out of Monopoly on the first day, as he kept winning; he'd had enough, anyway. He has an incredibly high IQ and is very interesting to be with. Yesterday we explored the ship. Andrew figured out a way to lose our robot so we went through to the rest of our deck.

Nothing there. It looked like an unused bay of cabins so we continued to the next section. We peered through the window in the communication doors and silently observed. Nothing going on.

Finally we braved it and slipped through the doors, and found stairs at the end of the corridor. We cautiously went down to the floor below and peered through these doors. There were some old people together talking in small groups: husbands and wives, friends? Don't know. You don't see old people on Mars so maybe they are all shipped back to Earth, so they can be looked after when they are ill or infirm. I think that's rather a nice thing to do. I'd like to imagine my grandparents enjoying their retirement. They left when I was very little on a ship just like this one. Maybe even on this ship – wow, there's a thought!

Suddenly there was a robot coming straight towards us, so we legged it back to the others, we didn't want to get into trouble. Mind you, when we walked in everyone was talking and busy with the game, so we nodded to each other and ran back again to the other end of our corridor. Someone came out of one of the rooms and disappeared towards the stairs. When all was clear we crept through the door.

I am ashamed to say that we took a bit of a liberty. You see the first door on the left was open so we went inside, having received no answer to our knock. We were looking around, not being that nosey, not opening cupboards or drawers or stuff, just walked through one room into the next. There was a voice behind us asking who we were and what we were doing. We apologised profusely (my Mum would have been proud of me, well not that proud as she wouldn't have approved of our disobeying rules and being there in the first place).

Not really knowing what to do we introduced ourselves and politely shook hands; it seems crazy now. His name is McKenzie and he was interested to know who we were and why we were on this ship. We talked to him about my abnormalities and he seemed to understand, but all too soon we had to go; there were the robots to consider. Andrew reckoned we should have about an hour before we were missed and that was just about up, so we scooted back to the main lounge and sat watching the stars.

We're going back tomorrow to talk to our new friend. Maybe some of the others, too. They might be able to tell us more about Earth. I don't know why we are kept apart, it would be nice to meet them.

Next afternoon (yesterday) we made our way down to level 2, the one below us, again. When we arrived there were several elderly people shuffling in pairs along the corridor away from us and we didn't get a chance to say anything. Four robots were guiding them along, almost ushering them. I wasn't sure they all wanted to go, but they did. It gave me the creeps, so we went back upstairs. Mackenzie wasn't there either. We waited as long as we dared but to no avail. We'll try again tomorrow. There are too many guards around in the evenings to get away.

I didn't sleep well last night. Not sure why but I kept thinking about that line of old people. Somehow I could feel they were sad; I couldn't get them out of my mind.

I woke early and wondered if Andrew was awake too so I got up to find his cabin. My door was locked. I don't know whether it is locked every night, or just last night as I've never tried to go out early before. But I was annoyed that I'd probably have to wait until the first pill buzzer to see him.

It has given me a chance to read over my notes and do a bit of editing. It's a simple log of my first interplanetary journey although I haven't written every day.

I can't stop thinking about those people. When I talked to Andrew he felt the same. Previously we've waited until afternoon before dodging the guards but we decide to try earlier today.

It's mid morning and the atmosphere in the lounge is different. I can't quite say why, it just is. Something has changed. My glance towards Earth ensures me that we are still on course and the Monopoly mob are hard at it – don't they ever get bored? Our sightless duo sit together with their helpers playing games or being read to. They have to be babysat all the time. Could be their operation is to restore their sight, I hope so. It must be awful not to see anything. I wonder if they have dreams or imagine things?

Perhaps because it's now our sixth day the sameness of everything is taking its toll. I look again at the Universe. Andrew is very quiet, I wonder what he's thinking.

"Right, Jay," he suddenly indicated. "Now's our chance. Move slowly to the side door so's not to attract attention."

It's worked! Free at last we headed for the far section of our level and down to the floor below, peering through the doors as before. No-one was about, the whole corridor was deserted. There weren't even any robots cleaning. There had been a lot of passengers here, a couple of dozen, maybe more. Where can they all have gone? Maybe MacKenzie had the answer.

We doubled back to his quarters, the door nearest to our end of the corridor, and were relieved to find it once again unlocked. We felt sure he wouldn't mind us waiting for him inside so we went in and sat down. He never came back, at least not before we had to leave. Our questions would remain unanswered. We had taken precautions and brought pencil and paper with us so left him a note, and then returned for second pill.

Something odd is definitely going on. Moraise and Saleena, the twins, are not in the lounge. We don't like to ask where they are or how long they've been gone in case they twig that we were missing. Andrew thinks it better to leave going back to see MacKenzie until tomorrow, the robots may be on some sort of alert. Mind you the twins can't have gone far on their own, can they?

2

Strange reply

Thursday, May 17th 2265

I have made a decision, this is going to be a proper diary so I have reverted to my normal format. There is something telling me that I should keep it hidden, and I don't think I'll even tell Andrew. Not yet anyway. I've devised a really clever password to hide it. My Mum is fanatical about passwords. She says too many people use birthdays or significant names or numbers. Mine is complete nonsense, but then, if you're reading this, I guess you've managed to crack it!

We've been travelling for a week now and I have a feeling it's important to keep a correct record of what happens on this strange ship. And it is strange, nothing feels real. It's like living in a dream – I openly admit to having pinched myself more than once.

At first pill we asked about the twins. No one else seemed to know anything, only that they disappeared mid morning yesterday. We asked the guards but, being a cog of robots, they are only programmed to say certain things, don't answer questions or enter into unnecessary conversation. We didn't even bother to ask 'The Morons' as we have nick- named the other group. They never talk to us, but they do join in with Monopoly. Andrew said that we should go and find MacKenzie, so that's what we did as soon as possible after pill.

It's annoying; even though we only eat pills and drink water we still have to sit there and make polite conversation for thirty minutes! Why? I can't see any point at all, except to delay us and probably give MacKenzie time to disappear again!

Eventually we are knocking on his door. There is no answer but it is unlocked. He's not there, of course, but we look for a note. It took a bit of finding but eventually Andrew looked in his reader by the bed and there, folded into the cover, was our note, with a reply on the back. Meaningless numbers:-

810.17156213719176198161921232223217.11158172
219156822

It was disappointing to say the least.

"OK, think sideways." This was Andrew. I sometimes wondered if I contributed anything at all to this friendship.

"Sideways?"

"Yes, Now he's obviously used some sort of simple code…," he sat on the bed and took out a pencil and began writing.

"Andrew? This could take some time. I think we should return to the lounge. We don't want to be caught here."

"You're right. Of course you are. Getting carried away. Come on!"

In fact we had been longer than we thought and it was almost noon when we got back to the lounge. We didn't sit in our usual corner to look at the note, but joined the others at the pill group. We'd have to wait;

the suspense was killing me!

Because of my deafness we have devised a simplified sign language between us so we can converse without being overheard. Andrew's amazing. It's taken me three years to learn to sign and he picks it up in three days! OK I can still surprise him with a few movements but he has a knack of understanding everything. I wish I had his brain!

The twins are still missing. So is Delman, the boy in the wheelchair. Maybe he's in the bathroom. 'Pill talk' is very subdued. I suspect we're all wondering what's going on. Are we all going to disappear one by one?

Eventually Andrew and I retreat to our corner and Monotony, as we've renamed the game, continues – at least it will keep them away from us.

"Not A," signs Andrew, thoughtfully.

"What are you talking about?" I sign.

He signs back and I can tell he's feeling exasperated with me. I must try to keep up.

"Look at the numbers." The game's noisier now so he says this out loud.

810.1715621371917619816192123222322217.11158172 219156822

"The numbers represent letters, right? If he'd started his numbering at A, then the last letter is V. How many words do you know that end in a V?"

He had a point.

"I'll try J. (I didn't even ask why J.)

A little while later he said, "Although it would end with an E it would begin with Q, so we get Q S. C A O D. No, I don't think that's worth pursuing. I'll work on

M."

Trying not to appear too stupid I looked at his notes and the alphabet written three times with each letter numbered. I mentally kicked myself; of course!

"Ah, huh! Now we've got T to begin with and ending in H. Worth a try. I'm sure he wouldn't have made it that complicated, even for me!"

We worked together arguing a bit whether each was a single number or a two figure one. This was easier than it seemed because 1 and 2 were M and N, so we quickly came up with:-

TV.CARGOSECRETBEGIHNDNGS.WATCHEA RTH, which split into TV. Cargo, Secret and Watch Earth, with something odd in the middle. Within seconds Andrew's face lit up. "Split the two's!" He'd almost shouted. And there it was; TV. Cargo, Secret Beginnings. Watch Earth.

It was the last bit that caught my attention. I'd been waiting for the Earth colours to be visible. There was a vague blueness but nothing more pronounced, and trying to think back I knew that the tones hadn't changed in my head for days. Surely there should be some increase in volume or tonal variety as we get closer. Maybe I was being too forward and this wouldn't be noticeable for several more days; a week even. The whole round trip was, after all, three months

The players were quieter now.

He nudged me and signed for me to wake up and snap out of my daydream. Didn't I realise how important this was?

"Yes, of course," I replied. I didn't tell him my thoughts about Earth. He wouldn't have understood. "So, what does it mean?" The game became rowdy again so we abandoned signing.

"I'm not exactly sure but whatever it is is going on in the cargo hold. We have to go down there and find out. What's more time may be running out. Three of us have already disappeared. Who's next? You? Me? Hopefully it'll be Catalina or Wesley to give us a bit more time."

At that moment the door opened and Delman wheeled himself in.

"Hi everyone! Bet you thought I was a goner! Had a bad night and only just woken up. How's the Monopoly? Who's winning?"

"I amend that last statement, Jay. You never know, perhaps the twins are staying in their quarters. I still think we need to investigate."

The two of us had become expert at guard dodging so we soon found ourselves outside MacKenzie's. He was out but we didn't go in.

"Whatever the 'secret beginnings' are they must go on in the cargo area, agreed?"

I nodded, he continued.

"We have at least an hour so I think we should find out how to get down to cargo. Hell! We don't even know how many levels there are! This is a transport vessel, there could be a dozen or more levels. Come on, let's find an elevator."

The corridor was empty, as usual. We made our way as quietly as possible towards the far end and, almost out of sight, the elevator. It seemed safer to use the stairs so we ran down, taking care at each bend. The door to the next level down, where we'd been before was marked 2, so we continued to what we assumed was 1.

"We need to be on our guard, Jay, sloppiness will get us caught. Look! There are people living on this level. More wrinklies! Shall we go and say hello?"

Andrew had turned to me to say this and get my opinion. Suddenly the door opened and a mechanical voice said,"Return to your quarters!"

He was obviously good at thinking on his feet because Andrew replied "Yes, of course, immediately!" He pushed his way through the door into the corridor as if he owed the place. I followed as he knocked on the first door on the left and went in.

"Oh heck, we're in trouble now."

"No, just keep your head. That robot didn't know who we were, now he will assume we live here. Luckily I don't think anyone else does."

I looked around and sure enough there were no personal belongings in this room, the bedroom or the bathroom. Just as well.

H e put his head out of the door. The robot had gone and the corridor was empty.

"Run!"

We made a dash for the stairs. "Up or down" Andrew asked, and we continued down to Zero or what would be ground if we were not on board a ship!

It was quiet. There didn't seem to be anyone about and it was a different layout to the other floors. We watched, peering through the windows in the doors. Someone we recognised came out of one room and went into another.

"Andrew, I think that was one of the twins. But it can't be. There was no guide and she was looking around as though she could see!"

"Yes, I saw her, too. Look! There's the other one!

15

What's going on here? Has their sight been restored? But why aren't they together? They've gone into different rooms. Jay, that's not right. They were always inseparable; like they were stuck together with glue! I don't like this one bit. Let's get out of here."

I led the way back up the stairs to level three. We checked the corridor before running towards the other end, where our quarters are and on to the observation lounge.

Breathless, we rushed in and sat down. The others stared at us. Then asked accusingly   "Where've you been?"

"What've you been up to?"

"Why are you out of breath?"

"Just getting a bit of exercise, running up and down the corridor," Andrew retorted. "Chess?" he asked me nonchalantly then signed to warn me of a robot coming up behind me.

That was it for now and for the evening, so we watched a movie with the others.

3

Where are the twins?

Friday May 18th 2265

I tried the door early this morning and it was locked again. Didn't matter, by the time I'd showered and dressed it was first pill call.

Still no sign of the twins. After pill, we sat in our usual corner signing, silently discussing what we had seen yesterday. If the girls could see, why were they not here and why had the powers that be not waited until we landed on Earth to operate on them? That's why we were going there, after all.

"It's something about beginnings." Andrew chewed it over. "What happens at the beginning? What is the beginning? Who is the beginning? Where is the beginning? How can it be a beginning?"

"We know where", I offered, "in the cargo hold. MacKenzie said that much."

"OK. Something very odd is going on in the cargo hold. It's obviously secret…. And MacKenzie knows about it," he added, after a pause. "I think he might have been trying to warn us."

"Yes, but where is he now? Is he avoiding us? Maybe he's being prevented from talking to us. He seemed to know a lot about the ship, as if he'd been on it before. I wonder who he is? Do you think he works on the ship – part of the crew?" I was thinking out loud; signing of course. "What about those first two letters, T and V?"

"It's obvious! Transport Vessel! Are you a total idiot?"

Thanks, Andrew, I thought miserably, but didn't sign. It was belittling and I felt like sulking, but it would have only made things worse.

"Sorry, Jay," he signed, having probably read my expression. "Shouldn't have said that."

"It's OK, but I find it difficult to keep up with you sometimes."

There was a commotion in the Monopoly corner. Wesley was being taken out. Two guards had brought a wheelchair for him and were trundling him away. One of the morons took his place as if nothing had happened. Whatever was going on?

"I'm still getting my head round 'Beginning.' What is the beginning but birth? We can't be re-born." Andrew was not leaving this alone.

We'd been chatting for a while and it was too late now to try and visit the hold again; we moved to the chess table to take our minds' off it. Sometimes if you leave a problem and do something new, you can you can see things differently. Andrew was obviously not concentrating properly as I won.

This afternoon we slipped out to find Mackenzie. He wasn't around so we went cautiously down the stairs and stood watching the zero floor activities. There were several people in white coats walking around. Suddenly MacKenzie came out of one room and went into another. He had a white coat on too, so he must be staff or crew, an official at least.

One of the twins appeared and went into the room nearest to us; instantly we decided to say "Hello." As they're identical we weren't sure if this was Moraise or Saleena. Quickly, before anyone else appeared we dashed out and into her room, entering all casual-like, as though it was no big deal. She stared at us.

"Who are you?" she said. I know we'd never been that friendly but surely... Then I remembered that of course she wouldn't know us, she'd been blind. She would probably remember our voices though.

I said the first thing that came into my head. "Hi. We haven't seen you upstairs for a while and wondered if you were OK."

"I do not know you. I will not communicate with you! Go!" This was her weird reply.

I persisted. "Moraise or Saleena, I'm sorry but I can't tell you apart. We were worried about you. Can you see?"

"See what? Who is Saleena?" It was her voice but it was different, very precise, not robotic but almost, scary!

I looked at Andrew and signed let's get out of here, just as the door opened and MacKenzie came in. He was not pleased to see us, but said we had tripped an intruder alarm and must go quickly. Curiosity wanted us to stay but we checked the corridor and then ran back to the stairs.

"Andrew, I'm scared. She was weird. That wasn't Moraise."

He ignored me and ran up the stairs two at a time, muttering something that sounded like "Note."

I followed and we took refuge in my cabin. He charged through to the bathroom and pulled a crumpled piece of paper from his pocket. (We had previously decided that the bathroom was the only room that would not have camera's or listening equipment, thus making the perfect sanctuary for private conversation.) He showed me a note that MacKenzie had thrust into his hand as we left.

M2110AMMY1/4

Another confusion of letters and numbers.

Andrew sighed, "Three days to wait."

Then I caught on, "Monday 21st 10am, My quarters. What are we going to do for three whole days? Andrew, I'm scared. I don't understand any of this."

"You and me both, Jay."

We stayed talking for a while, mulling things over. Putting forward suggestions, airing ideas. It didn't really help, except to confuse us even more. Eventually we returned to the lounge and snide comments of the others.

The morons had taken over Monotony, Delman was playing some computer game or other; Catalina approached us.

"You two seem to be more adventurous than the rest of us. Do you know where the twins are?"

I didn't dare look at Andrew. My Mum always says I am a rotten liar, so I signed for him to answer. I needn't have bothered. He lived on his wits and replied,

"No, but they can't have gone far. Maybe, as they need constant attention they have been moved to the nursery. It would be a safer environment for them. They're such a quiet and gentle pair so they'd enjoy the company of little ones."

Quiet and gentle, I thought. Andrew, have you ever been to a nursery? We're not even sure there is one.

We'd assumed there was when we came aboard because of the families around, but after recent events we'd found only two groups; the wrinklies and us. Those families must have being saying goodbye to their relatives.

Catalina accepted the idea, thank goodness, and went to watch a movie.

I tried to think this through. Was this another clue? But we didn't know for sure who was on this ship. There may be several more levels above us. Just because we'd used the extent of those stairs didn't mean there weren't more elsewhere.

"We should have checked the elevator," I signed.

"Guess you're thinking the same as me," Andrew replied. "It gives us something to do for the next three days!"

We joined the others and watched the movie, but it was smeli-vision and wasn't very nice as it was set 400 years ago. One of the Dickens stories called Oliver Twist and depicted a horribly dirty England with horribly dirty people! Yuk!

I wonder what will happen tomorrow? Fingers crossed, it will be better.

4

Locked doors

Saturday May 19th 2265

After first pill it was difficult to get away as there were two extra guards with us. We played our usual game of holographic three dimensional chess before I told the guard that I wanted to lie down for a bit with a headache.

Andrew sneaked out, not even bothering with an excuse, to join me ten minutes later and we went through to the end of the corridor and stopped dead. There were people about, we could see them through the doors. Not the wrinklies but ordinary middle aged people.

"Jay, I'm losing my touch! These must be the staff quarters. That's why MacKenzie lives here and why we've never seen anyone around during the day. Assuming I'm correct, we don't stand much chance of getting through to the elevator this way. Not today, I think it maybe some sort of Saturday rest day. We've never explored the other direction, so let's go back and see what's there. There must be more than one set of stairs."

We ran back, passed the lounge and our cabins area to the doors at the other end. They were locked. Andrew looked at the key pad next to it and fiddled a bit but to no avail. We peered through the window into complete darkness.

"Oh, damn and blast!"Andrew's words, not mine. "We're scuppered!"

"Why don't we see what we can find out about this ship through the net? We can use the terminal in my cabin. Failing that there's always my e-Tec pad."

He followed me through the door and I sat at the terminal. "Now, this is the USS Temeraire, right ……. Not a lot here. A bit about it's history as a transporter ….. bla, bla …… when launched etc. Nah, nothing about it since 2250 when it was converted for 'Special Purposes.' It was regraded as 'TV.' You know, Andrew, I have a feeling TV is something special."

"Hmm, yeah, well. It doesn't really tell us anything new. You can only access what's on the ship's records from here. Try the e-Tec. No, that'll only log on to the same stuff. Come on, we'd better report for second buzzer before we're late."

So that's what we did, feeling very fed up and impatient for Monday.

Catalina missed pill and we found out she'd been gone since mid morning. Only three of us left now. Delman was battling with the morons and Monotony – maybe he was a moron too! I suppose I shouldn't have such awful degrading thoughts, but I'm just so frustrated with everything. We are getting absolutely nowhere.

As the extra guards had gone, it was easy to get out and back again to what we now called the 'staff' area. This time no-one was around so we made for MacKenzie's and knocked on the door.

We were surprised when he opened it.

"Hello! I thought it might be you two. Curiosity

caught up with you did it? Andrew, Ophelia, come in, sit down."

Andrew looked at me and raised his left eyebrow. I shrugged my shoulders and glanced reproachfully at him, signing quickly "Later". Then smiled sweetly at MacKenzie and said, "Mr MacKenzie.......?"

"Professor, actually," he interrupted.

"Oh, er, well – Professor MacKenzie, will you please tell us what's going on?"

The silence that followed lasted an age. I could hear my heart beating, maybe they could too. I shouldn't have come straight out with it – should have let Andrew take the lead, ask the questions.

MacKenzie's piercing, dark eyes looked straight into mine, into my soul, unnerving me.

Andrew realised I needed rescuing. "Yes, sir. Our fellow passengers keep disappearing and when we talked to Moraise yesterday she was a very different person. She didn't know us, and she could see."

"Yes," said the professor, "unfortunate that. She wasn't ready to meet anyone so soon." And then, after a pause,"You two make a good team, you know. You must work together. Ophelia, don't underestimate yourself."

We waited for him to continue.

"At this time there is nothing more I can tell you. Now, you must return to the others. When you come on Monday the guards will not stop you. On second thoughts, make it Tuesday, same time. Gives you another twenty four hours."

He stood, opened the door and dismissed us! That was that!

"Thanks for nothing, Prof!" Andrew was livid.

"Why won't he tell us anything? And what do we need the extra day for?"

But I was catching on to the idea of thinking sideways. A couple of things were buzzing round my head. "Do you know what? I think this is some kind of test. I think we have to find out the secrets of this ship, and then we have to tell the world."

"Don't be such a Drama Queen, *Ophelia!*"

I will not bother to record the scene that followed. Needless to say it was bitter and childish and resulted in our sitting in the lounge as far as possible from each other until dinner time. Delman delighted in remarking that the 'love- birds' have had a row! Complete with the whoops and silliness that I would have expected from him. I shall be glad when it's his turn to go.

As we sat down for evening pill Andrew signed an apology which I accepted after he'd repeated it twice, stressing the really, *really* sorry bit. (Nothing like a bit of grovelling!) We sat opposite each other talking silently. IIe'd been going through what I'd said and agreed with me. Maybe I did add something to this friendship after all.

"I've had an idea. At least I think I have. I'll tell you about it later." I signed to him.

He frowned." Tell me now?" he returned.

I shook my head and repeated, "Later."

Under the ruse of chess, I signed my thoughts. "This is an old ship, right?"

He nodded. "If they've been using the same entry code for the locked doors then perhaps the keys might be a bit worn. Maybe if we used a light …..."

"We might be able to work out the numbers!" Andrew finished for me. Good idea, Jay, but if it's more than four numbers there would be dozens of permutations; it would take too long."

"It might only be two or three, worth a try. My phone would show enough light."

Unusually there were only two guards this evening and they were by the Monopoly table, so we chanced it and, collecting my phone, went to examine the key pad by the locked doors. Four numbers were marginally shinier and smoother than the rest, 1,4,6 and 9.

"That's a shame, Jay. Too many options."

We unsuccessfully tried a few and then returned, crestfallen to the lounge.

"Exactly how many options are there, Andrew?" I looked at him thoughtfully.

"I think it's 16; four squared."

"No, you're wrong. Its four factorial, so its twenty four...... How long is it really going to take us to press four numbers twenty four times?" He was interested now. "We might hit on the key quickly, but even twenty four times isn't going to take more than five or six minutes. Ten at most! Come on lets have a go."

In reality it was the eighteenth set of digits that worked, 9164, and had taken seven and a half minutes. The doors opened and the lights came on automatically, as before when we'd entered other areas. Another corridor which led to, you've guessed it, an elevator and stairs. With fingers crossed we called the lift and soon the doors opened. We both had the same idea and stuck a foot out together to prevent closure, mine stayed.

"We were right, there is another level, but it's not up. There's a second basement. See, look – 3,2,1, then Hold 1 and Hold 2. How strange. Now why would there be two cargo levels?"

26

"Because it's a transport ship?"Andrew mocked.

"Was, but it isn't any more. It was re-designated in 2250 …..."

Andrew was getting philosophical again, he eyes began to glaze over, so I reminded him that we must get out of here before we're caught.

"They don't need the cargo space any more so why not use it for more accommodation? "

I was getting nervous."Maybe they didn't change the indicator buttons on the lift during the refit. I don't know and right now I don't care either! Let's go!"

"Yes, but….."

"Andrew……..OUT!"

Finally we joined the others.

Before the film started I whispered, "No comment about the name?"

"Nah, sorry about that. I did wonder; is Jay your second name?"

"Jacaranda! My Mum studied botany, likes flowering trees, there's a beautiful one in the arboretum. Dad studied Ancient Literature. Ophelia comes from Shakespeare, apparently, but I'm usually called Jay."

"Fine by me, You should hear my middle name! Tell you later; no time now."

We swapped a look; eyes rolled – parents!

5

What's happening to everyone?

Sunday 20th May 2265

Andrew was waiting for me as I left my cabin.

"Euclid," he said,"Told you it was bad."

"Sorry, but I haven't got a clue what you're on about."

"My middle name, Euclid. My Mum's a mathematician. Geometry was her 'thing.'"

"Ah," I commiserated. "Well, I'll keep schtum if you will," and we nodded agreement.

"Jay, I want to say how sorry I am about yesterday. No, please don't interrupt, I need to say this. You see I've never had a proper friend before. Don't look at me like that – it's true, and I said some horrible things yesterday and upset you. At school I was always the swat who knew all the answers, kept myself to myself. No-one wanted to know me. Kids can be really cruel, you know. A form of bullying, I guess. But you're different. You've accepted me for who I am and I ruined everything! You're clever and funny and kind and gentle and I don't deserve you. Can you forgive me?"

"Of course, I already have. I haven't even written anything about it in my diary because I knew I didn't want to be reminded of it." Uh, oh, I thought, maybe he wouldn't notice. Fat chance!

28

"Diary? What diary?"

"It started as a log of my first trip on an interplanetary ship, but as we discovered strange happenings it turned into a diary. Nothing too grand," I said, trying to play it down.

"That's what you meant by 'telling the world.'" He'd switched to signing as a door opened behind us and Delman wheeled his way towards us.

"Hello, love birds!" he mocked. "You'll be late for pills if you don't stop canoodling!"

"Get lost!" We shouted at him.

"I wonder who'll be next to do just that," was his passing comment.

Andrew signed gloomily, "I hope it's him, not one of us. I can't imagine being here without you."

We walked towards the lounge.

"Listen," he said, "if I start going off on one just thump me or something; promise?"

"Andrew, shut up!"

Breakfast conversation was even more irksome than usual. We were all three together with the morons and not much was said at all, but it seemed awkward. At last they drifted off to the monotony of 'Monotony' (I like that phrase!) so we sat in the corner, more thinking aloud than chatting. The game was boisterous, so we didn't need to sign.

"I still want to know why there are two basement levels. The twins were in the upper basement. They apparently weren't ready to meet anyone yet, so could this be a recovery or rehabilitation section? Like the convalescent hospital on Mars. They didn't look ill, though, just....... odd, almost vacant. Like they were there in person but not in reality. I don't think I'm expressing myself very well; you're better at that sort of thing, Jay. There were people in white coats, who could have been doctors. Mind you everyone wears white so what's the difference?"

"But it wasn't the basic uniform-type clothing from Mars." This last comment was mine.

"Hmm. It's no good, Jay, we can't just sit here for two days wondering what's going on. We have to make an effort. I vote we go back downstairs. We can see who's around on the other floors. There might be chance to talk to someone, you never know."

I had been thinking about MacKenzie's first note. "Do you think this is part of MacKenzie's secret beginning? We never did solve that conundrum. I have a feeling that's the key to everything."

"Huh! You and your feelings! ….. OW!"

I'd punched him playfully in the arm. "Sorry, didn't mean to hurt."

"No, you were right and you could be right about the secret beginnings bit, too. Been a bit too single minded. Let's get out of here."

We were soon through to the staff section and this time there was no-one about. Saturday's the main rest day on Mars, so it must be the same here. The Prof's rooms were empty but he'd left an open message for us on the table. It said 'Not before Tuesday'!

He obviously expected us to come looking for him. We carried on to the stairs and down to level two. No robots, no-one. Then feeling brave, or foolhardy, we looked into the other rooms along the corridor – I call them rooms but of course they were suites, all with at least two rooms and a bathroom. Beds were made, everything was clean and tidy and no sign of anyone living here at all. We must have been unlucky when we met that robot last time, I thought, although I'm sure I remembered seeing people in this section before. We went up one side and back down the other, thus ending up at our stairs.

"Onwards and downwards?" asked Andrew. And so to level one where we had observed the elderly people walking and talking together. Was this yesterday? I tried to remember, no, I think it was the day before. I'm not sure. I'll look back in my diary later. (I did and it was last Thursday.) We went back into the room we'd gone into before, still empty.

Level one was deserted. Nobody appeared to be living here either. Where have they all gone? Again we checked all the rooms, before going down to the last level on these stairs, zero, or as we now knew, Hold One.

We watched through the door windows as Wesley came out of one room and walked, completely unaided, into another.

"They must be operating on everyone here, on the ship. But why bother to take us all the way to earth in that case?" I'm not sure why I signed this, but it seemed appropriate. I was sure we'd be in real trouble if caught.

Andrew replied, "Perhaps the other's problems can be rectified on board and you have to go to Earth. Maybe you're more complicated."

I read his response and I knew I had to put it out of my thoughts. There were a lot of ideas buzzing round my brain, secret beginnings, the morons, Earth, and I needed time on my own. Andrew was signing something that I completely missed and had to ask him to repeat, which, grudgingly, he did.

"Shall we follow Wesley?"

"No, Andrew, not now. It must be nearly noon. We've been gone for ages. We should go back and return later."

He agreed and followed me upstairs and through to the lounge, where the five morons sat alone watching a program on the television.

The Monopoly set was packed neatly away for the first time ever. Delman was gone and I couldn't help feeling relieved.

Surprisingly, lunch was easier than breakfast. No-one spoke and I felt no embarrassment about it. By no one I mean the morons; Andrew and I signed a few derogatory remarks, which we probably shouldn't have and eventually the half hour was up.

During this quiet time I had started to regroup my thoughts and decided to tell Andrew, so we left them to the telly and went to my cabin and sat in the bathroom to talk.

"Andrew, I need to ask you something very personal."

He seemed puzzled.

"Have you any idea why you are on this ship? I know that sounds silly, but everyone else has a disability. For want of a better word, is," I hesitated, "is there anything 'wrong' with you?"

"Other than my amazing brain?"

"No, come on, please, be serious. I'm trying to work something out."

"Sorry. I always seem to be saying that, don't I?" He paused to think, "No, I don't think so. The only thing is my brain and my high IQ. I know it's abnormal, but why would anyone want to change that?"

"I thought that, too. I can't work out why you're on a hospital ship. We'll have to come back to that. Next. Now, tell me why did we call the morons, morons?"

"Because they are!"

"Come on Andrew, *please* cooperate, I need help here, I need your input, and please don't say sorry again! You're always telling me to think sideways."

"OK. Well, they are dull and moronic and all the same…….. Oh gee whiz! Are you thinking what I'm thinking? Are they androids?" He said, excited now.

"Oh you clever girl! Why didn't I think of that. That's why they have packed away that stupid game. But why are they with us. Are they here to watch us? No, we've got the robot guards for that…….. Do you remember when they came with the wheelchair for Wesley and one of them slipped into his place at the table for continuity? Could that be their purpose? To keep things in the lounge running smoothly until we've all gone?"

"But they always leave us alone. Why?"

"Because we're special?"

"Are we here for a different reason?"

"And why are you here at all? I mean, I know why I'm here because of my hearing. They are wanting to operate so I will be able to hear better – at least, I think so. My mother signed all the forms so she must know the details. Hey, guess what? I'm eighteen on Tuesday; I can make my own decisions! How can I have forgotten something so important?"

"Mine was Feb. We'll have to celebrate. Tuesday? Everything's happening on Tuesday. Why did MacKenzie put us off till Tuesday? You could ask *him* about your op. I bet he knows."

"Andrew, we're getting side-tracked. I'm still trying to work out why you're on this ship. All I can think of is that you're here to keep me company!"

"Now who's being big headed!"

"I know, I know, but can you think of a better reason? The androids have never spoken much to us or taken any interest in us." I looked at him, thinking he's not going to like this next question. "Andrew, my dear friend, are *you* an android? I know so little about you except that your brain's the size of a planet and you come from Mars!"

For a moment he looked as if he was about to explode. Then he smiled and burst out laughing. "Now there's a thought. Brain the size of a planet, eh? Where did you get that one?" He came over to me and took my hands. "No, my sweet Jay, I'm as human as you are – well maybe not so humane, but yes, I am a real person. Now, I think we should sit in the lounge and relax for a bit. I could teach you Monopoly?"

He dodged my fist and we went back towards the observation lounge.

As we entered, faces turned towards us. Five unmemorable faces. They were individual, male and female, different shapes and sizes. But they had a sameness of character and I was certain now that they were androids. From his raised eyebrow I knew Andrew agreed.

As we settled down to choose a film Andrew smiled, "Where did you get that planet thing?"

From a book I read years ago. There was a character called Marvin, who had a brain the size of a planet and was terribly depressed. They called him the paranoid android!"

"Well," he grinned, "For Pete's sake don't start calling me Marvin!"

6

The evil machine

Monday 21st May 2265

Monday morning and our last day to find out the truth. Why should I think it's the last day? And why do I assume that everything happening on this ship is sinister? In some ways I don't want to know what's going on. I have a feeling that it will change my whole life. Andrew would laugh at that and I suppose I must now stop thinking and writing nonsense and go and join him. Perhaps he's feeling more upbeat than me and will cheer me up.

We met in the lounge. We were the only ones there; no androids, no guards and, of course none of our former passengers. We talked freely over breakfast, nice to be able to do that for a change, thinking aloud and revising what we have found out so far.

"Not very much," I listed things as they came into my mind.

1. Our fellow travellers have disappeared one by one (except the twins, of course).

2. They have had some kind of treatment for their disabilities – at least the twins and Wesley have, and Moraise behaved very strangely when we spoke to her. "We should have gone back yesterday and talked to Wesley. Why didn't we? Oh, yes, I remember. Too busy

talking, we shouldn't have wasted that time!"

3. The five moronic nursemaids are probably androids."

"And the older people that we've seen have all gone." added Andrew, "Where? Why? How?"

"Well, I don't see why we should stay here for the full half hour, so why don't we go and find Wesley?" Andrew suggested, getting up as he spoke and, as usual, leading the way.

The only corridor we were wary of was the staff one, but it was empty, so we continued down to the Hold 1 level. Nobody was around so we opened the doors and sneaked through.

A bit too blasé for my liking, he opened the first door. There were signs of occupation but it was empty. We tried the next. Wesley sat drinking a glass of water; probably just had his breakfast pill. He stood, unaided, and walked towards us. He smiled – that was a good start – and then said in a very peculiar voice, "Hello, my name is Wesley. Will you be my friend?"

We looked at each other. Not again. Thinking on his feet Andrew replied, "Yes, of course! Have you been here long?"

This seemed momentarily to confuse him. Then he repeated, "Hello, my name is Wesley. Will you be my friend?"

"We have to go somewhere first," Andrew again,"and we need to find some others as well." Then, as an afterthought, "Do you know anyone else on this floor?"

Again Wesley seemed confused. "Do you live here, too? I have seen other people, but not you or her."

His voice was very strange. Not robotic, nor as an

android would pronounce things, but stilted, unreal, almost like someone speaking a script for the first time. As Moraise had been last Friday.

I signed for us to go, so we said goodbye and closed the door behind us, not even checking who was outside. Luckily no-one.

Delman was in the next room, he was lying on a bed and looked to be asleep so we didn't disturb him. Next room along, Catalina was drawing, with the twins sitting next to her. We cheerily barged in saying "Hello," with Andrew continuing,"how are we all today, then?"

As one they turned and stared. Together the expressionless twins asked us who we were, but Catalina smiled; "I am very well, thank you, and how are you?"

Again those awful unreal voices.

I'd had enough. Also I'd had a really horrible idea. It was Andrew's fault -all this trying to get me to think sideways – and I didn't like it, the idea that is. I needed to talk it through with him. Maybe he was thinking the same. He was carrying on some inane conversation with Catalina; the twins were ignoring him. I signed that I wanted to go, now; it was important.

Outside I continued signing to ask where we should go to talk.

"Your cabin," he answered, "if that's OK by you."

Sitting on the floor of the bathroom, he asked me what was up.

"Is this one of your feelings again? No, I'm not mocking you, I promise. I know better than that now. What is it."

"Andrew, I'm probably wrong, in fact I hope I am,

but let me run this past you. All four of the teenagers we've just seen were weird, right? To look at they were identical to those we'd known in the lounge, right? Wesley even had that mole on the side of his face, so we know it was him. But *was* it?"

"It certainly wasn't him speaking; his voice but not his words, or any of the others for that matter, if you see what I mean? They were like ….. Oh, Jay, you're not thinking….? No, they can't be. *Clones?*…… But it takes years to make a clone. I mean they can't clone teenagers – can they?"

We sat and talked about this for a long time, not reaching any conclusion but voicing our suspicions. The main problem was that if they were clones, how had it been done? Unless they had been cloned soon after birth, and that seemed too far fetched. The whole idea made me shudder, and frightened.

"We still have no idea what happened to the older people." Andrew's mind was working overtime. Once he'd had the idea planted in his head there was no stopping him. "They wouldn't clone them, would they? What for? It would be like a rebirth……..This must be what The Prof meant by the Secret Beginning."

"Andrew, we've been here for ages, I think we've missed lunch. Although if nobody else is around I expect our pills and water are still there. Come on, let's go find out."

We sat with our drinks on our own. As we'd guessed pills were on the table.

We both needed a distraction so chess was in order. This time we used a different table, one where we could both gaze out at the universe. Neither of us could face any more 'adventuring' that afternoon.

"Jay, wake up! It's your move."

I apologised and without really thinking moved my bishop. Andrew groaned.

"Do you want to take that again? You're not concentrating. You're not having another of your 'feelings' are you?"

I snapped out of my daydream and replaced my bishop, moving my knight instead with a "Check!" to my satisfaction.

"Big mistake!" gloated Andrew. He promptly took my knight and I was in trouble, my king in check. Two moves later he'd won the game.

"Well, that was a waste of time!"

I said, "Sorry, do you want to play again?"

"Not unless you're going to concentrate and play properly!" he grumbled. "You know, we haven't investigated the second hold yet. The other staircase might go down that far. Shall we see?"

Did I have a choice? I certainly didn't want to tell him why I was in my daydream and what I was thinking about. Maybe I'd tell him later, but not now. It could wait.

Andrew entered the numbers sequence for the doors and we found the new stair-case. We ran down, being careful as we rounded the bends. Luck was with us and we saw no-one.

We stopped at the first hold level and peered through the window. A 'doctor' looking chap appeared, came towards us, but then went into another room. Was it too dangerous to go in? After a bit of signing we decided not to bother, we'd had our fill of weirdos this morning. Besides, the lure of the lower hold level was dominant. Cautiously we descended to unknown territory, and peeped through the doors.

The lights were all off so we concluded that the coast was clear. I suddenly remembered something that MacKenzie had said the first time we found Moraise, although it hadn't happened since.

"Andrew, MacKenzie said he knew we were about because we'd tripped an intruder alarm, will that happen again, here?" This I had signed and there followed a short conversation about the odds of getting caught and whether it was worth it.

"We'll certainly be trapped if anyone comes, maybe we can hide somewhere. Oh come on, Jay, we've waited so long to find out what goes on down here," he pleaded and I must admit I was curious. What can they be hiding?

The light came on as we entered, and I thought that if we were going to get caught it would be now. Nothing happened, at least no audible alarm bells. We stayed by the door for almost a minute, just in case we needed a quick getaway. All clear, so we started to look around. It didn't take long.

This area was a lot smaller than the other floors. We went through the only door. A small room with four doors leading off. We chose the first on the left, as usual. A room about three metres square. In front of us was a glass cubicle, not very big, a bit larger than the average shower.

Before I had a chance to take it all in Andrew grabbed my hand and said seriously, "Out, Jay, now please."

He wasn't abrupt or bullying, only firm, authoritative. I followed him, back up the stairs to my cabin. He'd gone very pale and I asked him if he was going to be sick.

"Not sure. Don't think so."

I ran to the lounge and got him some water, which he drank gratefully.

He lay on the floor of the bedroom to recover while I waited for him to explain. He was totally shocked and it took a few minutes.

At last he started. "I'm not good with words, Jay, you know that but I'll explain as best I can."

I sat and waited, wondering what was coming.

"It's difficult to know where to begin. As you know my Mum's a mathematician, My Dad is a development engineer. He invents things, no, he develops other people's ideas, turns them into reality." He shut his eyes for a while. "Oh, how do I tell you this?"

I could feel his awkwardness, even fear.

"About five years ago I needed some information for a school project. I was using his pc as mine was blocking stuff I wanted.

"I came across some work he'd been doing on a machine very much like the one we saw. Jay," he hesitated and then grasped my hand, making me nervous. "Jay, what we saw was a vaporiser!"

I stared at him, not knowing what he meant. I had wondered what a lone shower was doing in what obviously wasn't a bathroom, but what was a vaporiser? He looked me straight in the eyes and said, "It destroys things, Jay, anything. Simply vaporises whatever is in there."

A tiny voice from within me whispered, "Andrew, you mean the old people are…." I couldn't say it. Tears welled up in my eyes as I rushed to the bathroom and threw up, then sat on the floor, trembling. He followed me through.

"Oh no, no, no!" I blew my nose. "Andrew, we have to get out of here, we have to get off this ship!" He gave me a pathetic, and-how-are-we-supposed-to-do-that, look. I was about to tell him my latest theory when, for the first time since we had boarded, the tannoy came to life, bellowing for Miss Ophelia and Mr Andrew to return immediately to the observation lounge!

We obeyed and were surrounded by the morons. They were jostling us and all talking at once. We were individually challenged to chess and I won three times in a row. Then it was pill time and we were constantly chatted to about nothing. To Andrew I signed hopelessness, he agreed. We gave in and watched the film the androids had picked. We both enjoyed it; not surprising as it had been chosen to keep us occupied.

One of the morons came over with drinks for us and I downed mine before I caught Andrew's look of horror. So? I thought, if it's poisoned, so what?

7

Conversation with MacKenzie

Tuesday, May 22nd 2265

Morning

My 18th Birthday, and it doesn't feel at all different from any other day. I'd slept well, better than usual in fact, and felt cheerfully refreshed. Andrew was waiting outside my door.

"Happy Birthday!" he yelled and kissed me on the cheek! My first, except from family. For a moment he looked as embarrassed as I felt. I hope this isn't going to turn into some romantic liaison, at least, not yet. I surprised myself adding that last bit and tried to forget the idea. Today was too important to go there.

"I have a surprise for you," he laughed, loudly.

Another one, I thought as we made our way to the lounge. Luckily the room was empty as he climbed onto one of the tables and sang the birthday song. He then, from memory, recited at the top of his voice the complete Periodic Table, followed by every prime number up to 500 and the Fibonacci numbers to 5000!

"Couldn't think of anything else to give you! Happy Birthday, Jay. I say, do you think I could call you something else, something that's special to us? I wondered about 'Phillie.' What do you say?"

All this was said excitedly and in one breath. "Watch it or I'll call you 'Eukie,' which could easily become *Yukkie!* If I didn't know you better I'd have assumed you'd gone completely mad! Andrew, quieten down a bit, it's Tuesday."

"Yes. Yes, it is. It's your birthday and the day we have our interview with 'The Prof.' The day we find out if our theories are true."

"I didn't sleep at all last night," he went on, suddenly subdued, "That's why I revised the table and the numbers. Had to have something to do. Were you OK?"

"Yes, slept like a baby. That must have been a sleeping draught they gave us? You should have had yours too. You've got a suspicious mind!"

"Me! All those feelings and theories you've had!"

"Hey," I giggled, "only joking!"

"Hmm. Are we going to sit and twiddle our thumbs for the next hour or shall we go and see him now?"

He was halfway to the door as he said this, so I joined him and we sauntered through to MacKenzie's suite.

"You're early, though later than I expected. Happy Birthday, Ophelia." The Professor was welcoming and bid us to sit.

"Thank you, though, please, Professor MacKenzie, *please* call me Jay. No-one's called me Ophelia since the divorce and my father left. It has sad memories for me and Mum always hated the name."

Andrew frowned and signed that I'd not told him about my father, but I ignored him and listened to the

45

Professor.

"There are many things you don't know about each other, Andrew." This surprised us both. Could MacKenzie understand our signing? The Professor continued, "You will learn some of them today. But first, Jay, will you collect your colour glasses from your cabin as you'll need them later. And if we're being informal, I think you may call me Mac."

I departed to my cabin.

"Andrew," Mac looked him in the eyes and asked," what do you think of Jay?"

"She is the most amazing person I've ever met, and I want to spend the rest of my life with her!" (This he told me later and I blush as I write it in my diary. The glasses were a rouse as I didn't need them at all.)

I returned and sat, this time next to Andrew, to show solidarity. "You said You would answer our questions about the ship and what's going on. Today, Tuesday at 10am; so, fire away!" Oh no, why did I have to be so aggressive? I've blundered in again.

"Are, there you have me! But, as it is not yet 10 o'clock, perhaps you will begin by telling me what you have found out, or what you think you have found out."

Andrew nodded for me to continue, and everything came out in a rush.

"We think the others have been cloned, but don't know how. The morons are probably androids and you're killing all the old people!" I declared, with venom.

Andrew nudged me and signed. "You know you thought TV stood for something unusual? It does. Termination Vessel! You were right, again!"

"I can understand you, so there's no need to sign.

You are correct, Andrew, this is a Termination Vessel. I make no apologies, although I can't say it makes me proud to be in charge of such a ship."

"No more than I'm proud of my father for developing the Vaporiser."

"The morality of this fact should be put aside, it has nothing to do with the two of you, but is regrettably part of life as decreed by the Universal Guardians on Earth. It is not a subject for discussion and I will not enter into any."

We sat in uncomfortable silence.

"It took you a while to decide the lounge five were androids, which of course they are. I expect that was because you had so little to do with them. Your assumption that they are the peace keepers is correct. It was they who were given the task of reproducing that dreadful game of Monopoly, but I knew I had to devise something to keep the others busy and throw you two together, out of boredom if nothing else. It served it's purpose, and well."

"How do you know? How do you know when we discovered the androids?"

"We'll come back to that. You are again correct about the others from your group being cloned. When they return to their parents they will be perfect replicas of their original selves, but without their disabilities. The Guardians dislike imperfection. Life will be much easier and more enjoyable for them as ordinary able people. They will keep all their childhood memories but all knowledge of previous disabilities will have been wiped. A small memory adjustment for friends, neighbours and families will complete the task."

Mac said all this in such a cold, matter-of-fact way.

I was shocked and started to wonder what was in store for me, and Andrew. He read my thoughts but kept quiet.

"Why is Andrew here?" For me this was the most important question of all. Over and over again I'd tried to reason it out.

"You said yourself that he's here to keep you company."

This statement sounded alarm bells. "As simple as that?"

"Yes, and no. The two of you are very significant children." His hand came up and stopped our protests. "Yes, you are still children compared to your contemporaries on Earth. You have led extremely sheltered lives, so don't argue."

"Andrew is descended from two of the most important scientists of the twenty-first century, perhaps of all time, but his brain needs nurturing and training. Jay, your family lineage includes many writers, painters and philosophers. Together you are an amazing team. Do you know we have never had anyone else on board who has bothered to find out anything about the ship."

"I want to know how you know what we've been saying?"

"Well, Jay, a little confession. Since you embarked you have been under observation. Although you fooled me for a while, talking in the bathroom. We needed to be sure you had the tenacity and courage for the future."

"I don't like the idea of being spied on, although I suspected as much, hence the bathroom." That was Andrew and I agreed; I felt indignant, annoyed, almost betrayed and sat there fuming, while Andrew asked, "about the cloning. How can you clone teenagers? Surely clones start as babies, so they would have to have been cloned between fifteen and seventeen years ago?.......... Oh, no, I really don't want to believe this!" He'd answered his own question. "Is this what you did? As soon as a different baby is born you clone it, ready for the time when the changeover could be made. Am I right?"

"For someone who's not good with words, you are making an excellent job of explaining how things ....."

But, before Mac could finish I shouted at him,"Stop it! Stop it! Stop it! Stop quoting our private conversations to us!"

Mac apologised, changed his tone and began again. "Everything Andrew just said is true, although we wait until we are absolutely sure the abnormalities are permanent. Usually when the baby is about two, occasionally earlier, but not often. You know your mother has known about your colour and music problem since you were fifteen months, Jay, and so have we."

"Oh no, no NO! You're not going to clone Jay are you? No, I couldn't bear that, you'd have to get rid of me too!"

This outburst from Andrew surprised me, but then I thought about it the other way round and how I would feel if he was gone. Also I didn't like the way Mac referred to my colour music as a problem, a disability! My problem was my hearing, which was getting worse but not that bad. With my new sound enhancing devices I didn't miss much.

"Stop jumping to conclusions, both of you and listen. Because of your ancestry, because you are so special I have intervened. I am not going to allow you to be cloned. I hope this allays your fears."

Not entirely convinced, we let him continue. "I need to fill you in with some background. I have known both your fathers for many years. We were all at university together and have been close ever since. I never married but both of them did, resulting in you. You have been metaphorically betrothed since birth. Both fathers were enthusiastic and both mothers were not. We all thought that was that, but Newton-Aldrin is a comparatively small place and you may well have met by chance someday. Three years ago Jay's hearing began to deteriorate, and we saw an opportunity to bring you together, here, on the Temeraire. Judging from your feelings towards one another, I think we were right."

"Tell me, Mac, are there clones of us?" Cautiously, I'd asked the big one. Did I really want to know? I wasn't sure.

"I have already informed you that you are safe from replication, you must believe me. I am completely on your side in everything. Now, I suggest you go back to the lounge, have your pills and perhaps a game of chess or something. You need a break and I have to attend to someone. You may return in an hour, not before. And by the way the surveillance has been completely withdrawn, I promise you that. In any case it is no longer necessary. One more thing, your father gave me this when I last saw him. He said I was to give it to you on your birthday." He handed me a small package which, disinterested, I put in my pocket.

We skipped chess. I explained to Andrew that I needed to write up this morning while it was fresh in

50

my brain and he understood. Either I was getting better at lying or he needed quiet too. We'd heard so much and both wanted to think.

Transcribing onto my e-Tec took three quarters of an hour. I'm getting quicker at dictating. If Andrew was listening he never commented.

Afternoon

"You never said about your Dad leaving. Do you remember him? How old were you when he left?"

Andrew's enquiry was kindly meant, but I wasn't in the mood and dodged the subject by replying, "Isn't it odd the way they both know Mac. I wonder if our Mothers' have ever met? Mine's a complete computer nerd, by the way. Writes programs and stuff. I suppose maths comes into that, so they might have."

"What did Mac give you as we left? Did he say it was from your Dad?"

I removed the package, which had become strangely soft and squidgy in places. It was wrapped in purple paper and had a second cover of silver coloured material, not paper, but serving the same purpose. I waited while my brain quietened and then unwrapped it. "What is it?" I asked Andrew. It was brown and subdivided into smaller portions, it smelt different from anything else I'd known; not unpleasant. "I wonder what you do with it." It had started to melt so I wrapped it up again. We decided Mac would know, and we set out once again for his quarters.

He was waiting for us, so, before it melted any more, I showed him the present and asked him what it was for.

He laughed and said, "Eating! It's called chocolate, taste it. I think you'll like it."

I licked my messy thumb and, umm, yes, he was right. Andrew ran a finger over a melted bit and cautiously licked it.

"I could get used to this," he approved. "Is it readily available? Where did it come from?"

"Interesting reaction, young man. Now, where were we. Did you go through everything over lunch?"

"No, I needed to get my di.....Oh." Abruptly I stopped realising that I'd already said too much.

"Don't worry, I was sure you'd keep note of everything. Dear girl, you are a writer. I should not have expected anything else. A word of warning, though. Protect it with an impossible password."

"I have, one of Mum's foibles! May I ask about the clones? Sorry to go on, but the whole idea fascinates me, even though I don't think I approve."

"Ask away."

"If the clones are already aboard ship when we arrive, why is this trip taking so long? We have a three month schedule."

"Interesting observation. You've met Wesley, the twins and Catalina. Your impression was not favourable. In fact you knew almost straight away what they were. The answer to your question is very simple. They have to be socialised, turned into their original happy selves. Memories and personalities restored so that even their parents don't suspect the switch. This takes time, approximately ten weeks."

In the quiet that followed I remembered something, "Where is my father? I didn't even know he was still alive. What's he doing?"

"I wondered when you'd ask. I don't blame you for your hesitance, he left when you were four so it must be difficult for you. He is on Earth. A professor of ancient literature and is keen to meet you again. I will not say where he's based because I don't want to corrupt your judgement. You have some very important decisions to make, not least where you would like to live. This is why I deferred this meeting until today, your eighteenth birthday. Andrew, this is important for you too. Jay will need your help, she cannot manage on her own."

For a moment I thought we were about to be dismissed again, but, no, Mac continued to explain about our clones. "When you asked if you had been cloned, I wasn't exactly truthful. Your clones are here."

Not a nice thought, we looked glumly at each other. Again Mac held his hand for us not to interrupt.

"We needed to get you both on the Temeraire and, believe me this took some planning. Your mother, Andrew. believes you have a brain tumour. Not easy to fake tests, x-rays, and medical records. To all intents and purposes, you are at death's door and have been transferred to earth for lifesaving treatment. It seemed wrong to deceive such an intelligent woman, but it was the only way. Because she did not want you to know how ill you were, your mother signed consent forms, not knowing if she would ever see you again, That in itself was illegal as you were over eighteen. But, you had to be with Jay."

"Poor Mum," muttered Andrew, "she must have gone through hell; still is I guess."

"Yes, and you need to remember that." He looked at me. "Jay, your mother has been troubled by your musical abilities and confessed to me, without knowing

53

who I was, that she wished you didn't have this strange affliction." He saw my reaction. "I said you would learn a lot about yourselves today."

"I thought Mum was with me and my music, and as for Dad, well! I am so confused, I want to scream!"

"Hold on for a little while longer. The reason you are here in this office is because I have to ask your permission to activate your clones and send them back to Mars in your place."

Stunned silence.

"Not sure I understand" Andrew looked as dumbfounded as I was. "What's going to happen to us?"

"We are offering you both the opportunity to go to Earth. To study, learn and become important members of the community. We can help you with the transition to earth life, and chocolate! Triviality aside, this is what you must consider. Tomorrow we talk again and I will show you what life will be like for you on Earth. Such a momentous choice, but you have only two days to decide. On Friday a shuttle leaves Mars to rendezvous with the United Star Ship Endeavour and you will need to be on that if you are going. There will be no return to Mars, ever, as your clones will have assumed your identity.

"Go now and share your thoughts. Tomorrow we can go into more detail. May I suggest, Andrew, that tonight you take the sleeping draught. The drug is very mild and harmless, but will give you much needed sleep. Get rid of those heavy rings round your eyes." As we turned to go he handed me back the chocolate, "Enjoy this while you talk."

Evening

The chocolate was wonderful. We didn't eat it all but saved some for later. For a while we just sat in silence, privately going over the days' revelations. Then Andrew got up and fetched pencil and paper.

"We need to be logical about this," he declared.

"I think what we should ask ourselves is 'Do we want a new life, on Earth and probably together?'" It felt weird saying this, but I think I was right.

"Either we go home as if nothing had happened, me as a clone, maybe you too, although for the life of me I can't think why they would need to clone you!" I caught Andrew's expression. "Sorry, I don't mean that in a nasty way. It's just that there's no reason for you to be replaced by a clone." I rambled on.

"It seems you are the important one, Mac said that, and I'm here to help you, so I think the decision is yours. Whatever you decide, I'll fall in with!"

"Andrew, no, that's so totally undemocratic! Let me put it another way. Do we want to live on Mars or Earth? What do you want for the future?" I looked straight at him and he grinned, a pathetic, ridiculous grin! Be serious, I thought and closed my eyes. When I opened them again his expression had changed.

"It certainly would be nice to go to Uni, but couldn't we do that anyway, here later. I know there's one in Newton-Aldrin but maybe we should be aiming higher? I've heard of Harvard and Yale and I believe there's somewhere called Oxbridge? There must be loads of others. If we go back home we shall probably spend the whole of our lives on Mars. And end up back on this ship, oh no! What a horrible thought!" He paused, obviously thinking about this prospect.

"Jay, do you remember when we had our row? You'd said about telling the world what's going on here. Well maybe it's not such a bad idea. Surely the general public can't know that everyone is vaporised at the age of ......He didn't say, did he? Right, paper pencil; we need a list of questions to ask."

He wrote, asking, "How old are you allowed to live, no, when do you die is better?"

"How about, 'At what age is life terminated?'"

"Perfect, Jay. Here, you do this, you're so much better with words than me."

So, beginning again I wrote:

1. At what age is life on Mars terminated?
2. What will our Parents be told if we go to Earth?
3. Can we return to Mars without being cloned?
4. Go to Uni there?
5. If I go home what about my colour music?
6. Andrew's father, what does he know?
7. Will we have any memories of this trip at all?

"These ideas are all very well, but do they matter?" I sighed. "Surely we should consider our parents, too. From what Mac said, your father may be in on this and mine definitely is, hence the chocolate. Do you think there's an inexhaustible supply on Earth? Sorry, me being silly this time! Andrew, your mother will be pleased to have you home and apparently fit and well. Could you cope with living a lie? And now you know your father's involvement with the Vaporiser and seen what they use it for, could you live with that knowledge; live with him? I'm not sure how I feel about my mother's revelations about my colour music. I had hoped she would help me transcribe it later on, but now it seems that would be an imposition on her and she wouldn't want to. Although maybe that won't arise as it could be taken out of my brain and certainly would be if I was a clone! Oh, dear, I'm so muddled!"

"Here,"said Andrew, handing me the last piece of chocolate. "You make the whole prospect sound so awful. But you're right about my Dad. I'm sure I couldn't keep the awful machine a secret for the rest of my life! Mac said it was nothing to do with us, but, in a way it's the most important thing."

The door opened and one of the androids arrived carrying our sleeping medicine, which, with nodded agreement we both drank. A definite decision to sleep on it and continue in the morning.

8

My theory

Wednesday May 23rd 2265,

Morning

I awoke to the sound of knocking. Andrew was calling me to get up, it was already eight.

"Give me five," I shouted back and jumped into the shower.

He greeted me as I entered the lounge. "Long five, almost ten, but I'll forgive you! Gather you slept OK? So did I; needed it; feel more alert." He was back to his normal abrupt self. "Here, had mine." He plonked the little container with my pill in front of me. I was surprised he hadn't waited, but not annoyed, after all it was only a pill and water. Two minutes later, he smiled, "Fit? Let's go quiz the Captain!"

"Yes, if he's in charge he must be; it never occurred to me. Andrew, have you decided what you want to do?"

"Nope! Fell asleep! Good thing too!" He was too smug, too cheerful. I knew something was amiss. He knocked on Mac's door. "Morning Cap'n!" Ooh Andrew, I thought, don't push your luck!

Mac hadn't minded that we were so early, I think he was pleased to see how enthusiastic we were.

I waited for Andrew to come out with something confrontational, and he did. There was no preamble, no intro, straight out with it.

"Two weeks ago we left Mars and have been travelling towards Earth ever since. If we have to be back on Mars for Friday, just how are we expected to do it?" With a satisfied smirk in my direction, he challenged Mac.

Mac looked at me. "Jay, would you like to answer that? I think you know."

I wished I'd had the sense and the forethought to broach this subject last night. Andrew was looking daggers at me as though I'd kept an important secret from him, which, in a way, I had. Gathering my thoughts, I tried to tell him. "Andrew, you know that when I see colour music forms in my head. We had to wait a few moments yesterday when I opened the chocolate because of it."

"What's chocolate got to do with transportation!" he retorted, grouchily.

"Nothing, I'm only trying to explain how sensitive my brain is to colour. Listen, *please!* I've not deliberately kept anything from you, I hadn't got around to telling you my theory yet. So much has happened in the last few days."

"Humph!" Andrew wasn't helping. Nor was Mac, sitting there listening. He could have taken over. However, at least now I was certain I was correct.

"I've only seen Earth through a telescope before now. I knew it was called the blue planet, as Mars is the red. So as it became visible I was excited and so looking forward to hearing the colours. But it hasn't happened. The Earth has stayed the same for four days

59

now. Exactly the same."

"Of course it has. It won't appear much bigger until we get nearer," he answered crossly.

"Andrew, you're not listening. I *know* there has been absolutely no change to the size of the Earth, because it has the same dull muted note, and has done since Saturday and maybe Friday as well."

"It's just too soon to be any different, Jay. There's weeks to go yet!"

"You know, Andrew for someone with a brain the size of a planet, you can be remarkably slow sometimes."

"So, the ship's stopped and we're hanging around in space?" Was his spiteful, sullen reply.

"No, dear friend. We never left Mars!" That silenced him and I looked to Mac for confirmation.

"Because of your unique abilities no one but you, Jay, could ever have discovered this. By the end of the first week cloning is normally completed and eventually the same film sequence is used in reverse. Your father said this would happen, and it was one of the reasons you have been given the run of the ship. Perhaps too much freedom. You were supposed to keep to these stairs and not discover Hold 2. I underestimated your chances of getting through locked doors! And I assumed you would remain in the lounge until later on Saturday. If you had, the staff would not have been around and you would not have needed the other stairwell. This reinforces our theory that you are more than capable of the tasks ahead of you.

Andrew was dumbfounded. He sat opening his mouth as if to say something and then closing it again, like a holographic gold fish! I mouthed, sorry to him and so wished I'd shared my theories earlier, but I hadn't been sure until a few minutes ago.

"Thank you very much, Jay!" he yelled. "I thought you were my friend! Am I to be forever kept in the dark, treated as an imbecile? I don't know where I am with you any more!" After this outburst, he stormed out of the room.

I knew he could be touchy, temperamental, but I never expected this.

"Go after him, Jay. He'll be OK, he's just lost face, that's all. And a bit of dignity. Come back when you're ready and we can continue."

All very well to say 'go after him' but where was he? The obvious place was the lounge, although I felt sure he wouldn't go there as it was too big to be private. I was right; empty, not even a moron. I tried my cabin, again without any luck. I'd never been into his cabin and wasn't certain which one it was. But then we were the only ones from our group on this floor so did it matter if I chose the wrong door? His was the second one I tried, maths and science books strewn everywhere, but he wasn't there.

Where would he go? Of course, the first suite on level one! Neutral territory! I ran down the stairs. As I opened the door he looked up and then away from me. Not knowing if this would be our second row or not, I nervously began, "Andrew, I'm really sorry, it wasn't intentional. It was an idea I had but didn't want to believe. I was so looking forward to going to Earth. I thought maybe if I ignored it, it would go away. I had almost convinced myself that it was too soon for the notes to change. Maybe the changes were so subtle that it hadn't registered. Perhaps in a few more days it would become more noticeable."

"No, Jay, it's me that's in the wrong here – again." He was calm now. "I do seem to be good at messing things up, don't I? Sorry about the shouting, Mac'll think I'm a right cretin."

"He won't. He understands a lot more about us than we realise, if that makes sense. My guess is that he'll never refer to the incident again. Shall we go back and find out some more?" I felt in my jeans pockets. "That's a shame, I've forgotten that list we made yesterday. Not that it matters but it would have been useful to check we'd asked everything." I thought for a minute and then said, "Something else you should maybe know – I have total recall. I think that's what it's called. I can remember conversations and things that happen word for word, with absolute accuracy."

"Wow!" I thought my memory was good! But what about yesterday when you needed to write your notes before you forgot stuff?"

"I know what you're thinking, and yes, it wasn't necessary, but I knew you would ask about my father and I couldn't face going into all that. Sorry."

"You can tell me all about it another time. Now, I think we should return to Mac."

He was waiting for us and didn't seem too bothered by the time we'd been away. I was right, Andrew's little episode was never mentioned.

He greeted us, holding out what looked like another packet of chocolate but this time the wrapper was red. "Try this," he suggested, it's a little more bitter than the last chocolate you had." This seemed to me to be an odd thing to do. Was it a peace offering or perhaps something to make us feel more relaxed and trust him. I thought about this. Do I trust him? I don't know. What do we know about him? He knows both our father's. He's had a conversation with my mother – face to face, video phone, whatever. He visits Earth, possibly frequently. He is in charge of this ship so must be the Captain, and several times he's said 'we, us and our,' who are they?

"Jay! Jay, wake up!" Andrew was waving his hand in front of my face. "Try this," and he thrust a piece of chocolate into my hand. "It's really good. I think I like it even more than the other one." He quickly signed, "Later, tell me."

If Mac read his actions he never said. Andrew always thought quickly, "I'm still interested in those clones, Mac. Logic has it that they must be two years younger than their – umm – originals, for want of a better word. And where have they been living for the last fifteen years or so?" He licked his fingers.

"Scientific achievement is a fascinating subject; so is the development, of the human brain. It has become possible over the last century or so to accelerate normal progression. Not by much. We needed only to gain those extra two years and nine months, but choosing the right time to do so is critical."

Mac was obviously happy to be back on this subject. I had no idea how right I was!

"One would assume that an infant's development could be increased during the first few months of life, but no, a small baby is growing and changing too quickly for this. After trials we now know that these two and three quarter years must be separated into two periods of eighteen and fifteen months. The ages of five and nine are the most advantageous for this accelerated development and learning procedure to take place. Thus the two, the clone and the original being, attain puberty together."

"It is enormously expensive and time consuming to bring each young person to the same stage as his or her model. We have direct and complete knowledge of their education, from their Mars tutors but, of course the child has no memories. Nothing at all personal. This is added at the time of the switch."

"Now it is time for you to return to the lounge and have a break. I have a meeting to attend and will be back here in an hour." He added, with a smile, "Take the chocolate with you; maybe Jay will taste it this time."

Alone in the lounge we sat silently with our water. As if suddenly remembering, Andrew asked what I was thinking when Mac handed us the chocolate. Perhaps it was the small package in front of us that reminded him. "What were you thinking about earlier? You were completely absorbed."

"Mac," I said. "I was wondering why he had given us this," pointing at the package and shutting my eyes. "Was it a peace offering? Was he trying to gain our confidence? Get us to trust him? Then I started wondering what we know of this man. He knows both our fathers. He has talked to my mum, although maybe not actually met her? He visits Earth and, I think, frequently. He's in charge of this vessel. Anything else?"

"He knows an awful lot about cloning," added Andrew. "Also he kept referring to 'us' and 'we.'"

"I'd picked up on that, too. Who are they? What's he part of? What do they want with us?" I was silent for

a while while digesting the implications. My mind a
multitude of questions.

9

Harrison MacKenzie

Mac opened his desk revealing a terminal and activated the iris scan, followed by a long complex pass code. He then evoked the scrambling device and keyed in a number. Holding the reply, he keyed in a different one; three way contact was established. Two images appeared on the split screen.

"Good morning Otto, James or should I say 'good afternoon as it is now after twelve."

This preamble was not merely a greeting, but to allow the recipients time to re-route and scramble conversation, authenticate identity and ensure absolute secrecy.

"Otto, your son does have a temper, doesn't he? I wonder who he gets that from?"

"Hello, Mac! His mother, of course! Over to you, what's new?"

"So far all is going to plan. Everything we predicted they have discovered, including the vaporiser, which I have refused to discuss with them, therefore making them even more curious and annoyed. They were incensed by the idea of it. Andrew's previous access to your notes usefully enhanced this, and may be a key point in his deciding to defect, although I am sure he will do whatever Jay wants. He is completely besotted, as we hoped. It's your daughter, James, I have to convince.

"They have not yet told me their decision, but I think they will agree, although I may need to reveal more of our plan, our dream to them but I shall use my judgement with this. It would appear they are not entirely adverse to cloning; the interest is there. They are a perfect team. Jay is lively and intelligent. She has the capacity to calm situations, to think things through and, even more useful, she has a natural way with words. The perfect peace maker. But she doesn't trust me. I must be careful, circumspect. A battle of wits, you might say.

"My successor is on aboard, but knows nothing of the real reason I am transferring. He has been told I have to return to Earth for an emergency. The Guardians will be informed after the event.

"Otto, James, we have discussed the children's transition to Earth life. This will be a problem, though not insurmountable. They maybe eighteen in Mars years but years younger in comparison with their counterparts on Earth, but with an extraordinary intellect. What was your old expression James; fourteen, going on forty? They have never been exposed to crime, greed, violence or even religion. There is none here, even on film. They have never even tasted food. The chocolate was well received, by the way, James, a good idea of yours. Because of this vulnerability I intend to keep them on board the Endeavour for a while, maybe up to a year, however long it takes, for them to be able to fend for themselves in a very hostile environment."

"I think that covers everything. Same time tomorrow?"

"Wait!" this was James. "Does she know about her relationship to Catalina?"

"No! And as far as I'm concerned she never will. Your philandering, James, has nothing to do with this project! Over and out!"

As he closed the terminal desk he was thinking about the Guardians. They had a lot to answer for in creating their experimental Utopia here on Mars!

10

Disclosures

Wednesday May 23rd 2265 - Later

We sat in the lounge, mulling over what had been said, both yesterday and this morning. We still hadn't broached our list of questions, which I now had, so we perused it together. Andrew muttered aloud as he read.

"Termination age? Parents told? Your hearing and visual music? My father's involvement? Local Uni?"

We added' 'Who does he mean by we?" But I'm unsure how we can ask this.

I should have known. In his usual blunt fashion it was the first thing he said as we entered the office.

"Who do you mean by 'we.'"

"Like your father, not one for niceties."

I had a feeling Mac was procrastinating.

"I should have thought you would have worked that out by now? Whom do you think is involved?"

Annoyingly he'd thrown the question back at us! Did he expect us to drop the subject? If he thought this, he had another think coming! I intervened.

"No! That's not fair, We're fed up with being 'played' by you like some ancient musical instrument! I don't know who you are. Professor? Captain? President of Earth for all I care! If you want our co-operation, which I think you do, then it's about time you were straight with us."

Uh, oh! Had I gone too far? I'd surprised myself at being so outraged, but I knew Andrew would agree with me.

"Ah, Jay, you are learning to be forthright! Trust your instincts and never underestimate your capabilities. I apologise, I did not mean to avoid the question."

Liar! I thought, that's *exactly* what you wanted to do.

"Sit down, and I will explain as much as I can. First more background. No, Jay," he held up his hand, to stall my interruption. "I am not going to fudge the issue, but it is important to be seen in context."

"I have already told you how I know your fathers. As students we were idealists. I suppose that's normal, every student wants to change the world. We had a lot in common, but mainly that we were all from Mars. Believe me the difference in lifestyle on the two planets is..... well...... very big."

The hesitation suggested he was searching for the right word. Was he trying not to put us off going there? Ignoring these thoughts, I told myself to listen.

"Our time, except at lectures, was spent together. We all attained double firsts, continued to doctorate and eventual professorship. Otto and James returned to Mars, entering into family life. Your father, Andrew, is *the* most important and talented development engineer of his time. Jay, yours is the world's leading authority on Ancient Literature. As you may have guessed my forte is neurology, both in development and surgery. Cloning is also a speciality.

"Surprise, surprise!" A hint of sarcasm in Andrew's

voice. "Are we to understand that the three of you are into some clandestine plot?" Blunt and to the point.

"In a way, yes."

Too straight and too honest, I thought, it can't be that. Stop it brain, give him a chance.

"We need to go back to the original colonisation of Mars, when Newton-Aldrin was first conceived, two hundred years ago. Earth had almost been annihilated after a third world war, which you will learn about later. It took decades to recover from the near total destruction of many areas and cities. During this time The World Council was created, to ensure this could never happen again, and the Guardians were appointed to their role as peacekeepers. They were desperate to create a world that was different, peaceful, and Newton-Aldrin was designed to be just that. A world completely without evil, crime, hunger, greed, religious adversities. A world where no-one would ever want to start a war."

"But, Mac, that's so unnatural. The old civilisations were always fighting, especially nineteenth and twentieth century Europe. Is it because of our isolation in Newton-Aldrin and the fact that no-one owns anything, not even their clothes that keeps the peace? Own nothing, so want nothing? If they built another city would it be different? Would residents then become rivals?"

"An interesting perspective, Jay, and one I would like to discuss with you another time. Now, to continue, our city was built and has been the desired Utopia for approaching a hundred years. The Guardians have become more obsessive in their demands for perfection. Otto's work on the Vaporiser was secret, although he always informed us of it's progress. This machine is

71

used only on this termination ship and is still Top-Secret."

"Before you had your little altercation on Saturday......."

Huh! I thought, nothing's private.

"Jay, you speculated about telling the world the secrets of this ship. You were right. That is exactly what we want you to do. Your fathers and I abhor the idea of this vaporiser and want to publicly denounce the Guardians for their use of it. We cannot do this ourselves, but hope that you can and will. This is the key to everything."

We sat in silence, while the implications of what he had said sank in.

"That's a hell of a prospect," Andrew looked at me. Underneath that practised, disinterested stare I sensed something else. Excitement? I couldn't be sure, but I knew what I felt; amazement mixed up with fear and anticipation.

I took our list from my pocket and glanced at it. I couldn't trust my brain to remember everything – it was too stunned. Except for my hearing and visual music, the questions were irrelevant. Andrew was still looking at me, he almost nodded.

"Professor," I wasn't sure why the formality. "Would you mind if Andrew and I had a break?" And then, "I assume that Otto, James and you are the only conspirators?"

"We are," he replied. "Return when you're ready, though please will you keep to the lounge/cabin areas. It is even more important now that you are not seen."

We opted for my cabin, the lounge seemed too big to be at ease.

"Andrew, I have a suggestion." I said this as we entered my cabin as usual. Why don't we each write down what we want to do; where we want to live and why? That way we can be sure of not influencing each other too much. Don't look so glum, only a few words, a dozen or so. You sit here and I'll go through to the bathroom, it'll make it easier."

I sat on the floor, thought for a moment and wrote:- Earth. Killing people is wrong.

Back in the cabin we swapped notes. Andrew had written:- Earth. Because I don't want to end up here!

We looked up. My eyes filled with tears. Andrew handed me a tissue. "Blow you nose. Decision made. We know 'where', now lets go and find out 'how.'"

Mac seemed pleased, if a bit surprised to see us so soon. We'd burst into the room, grinning like idiots talking together.

"We're up for it! We want to go to Earth and save the world!"

"You're certain?" he asked, so I handed him our notes. "Shall we go through that list of questions you were holding earlier?" He asked.

Andrew began. "You said you needed our permission to activate our clones and return them to Mars. Will they be, like…... normal people? Will our parents know who they are?"

"Your mothers' will be told nothing of the changeover and will have no idea you have been replaced. Andrew, yours will be delighted to regain her son, fit and healthy. Your father has kept this secret for sixteen years. Your clones will be your Martian selves and have good and fulfilling lives there."

He turned to me. "You need to consider another

aspect of this. Your colour music gift. It can be transferred to your clone, but, as I said, your mother would prefer it wasn't. Harsh, I know, but there are options. It can remain with you, but Earth is a kaleidoscope of colour. You can have stronger spectacles but would need to wear them continuously and would need to live without colour in your personal life, which I think you would find very difficult. There is a third option, to transfer your ability to someone else. Your hearing is to be corrected tonight, by the way. That's a completely separate matter."

"Does the alteration for my colour music have to take place then, too?"

"It can do, it depends what you decide."

"We became so obsessed with finding out about the Temeraire I'd almost forgotten my music. I was so looking forward to hearing Earth as we approached." A sudden sadness overwhelmed me.

"There is a film for you about earth. It covers different aspects including the planet as viewed from outer space." He stood and retrieved a tape from a drawer. "You may take it to the lounge on your own, or view it here, now."

Andrew quickly signed, 'lounge'- old habits die hard, I thought. I wasn't sure what to do.

"Why not take it with you. I am available this evening if you need me. Use this device and I will come to you. Go now, you have much to talk through."

It was too early for pills so we sat together on a sofa and watched the film. The first five minutes were wonderful! The planet Earth was so amazing, colours changing as we approached. Shades of blue and green, mixed in with yellow and brown and white as well. I have never seen anything like it, not without my glasses, that is. My head was so loud! I lasted through a piece about the oceans and dolphins, then the change to somewhere called India made me cry out in pain.

Andrew stopped the film while I calmed down. I didn't notice him leave the room, but then he handed me my glasses. "Wear these, then maybe I can describe the colours to you."

I appreciated his concern and optimism. The film continued, but without the narrative and Andrew's inept, monologue descriptions, I became so confused.

"Can we go back to the beginning?" The sounds began so beautifully, so subtle and calming. But I pressed 'pause' after only a few minutes.

"Andrew, I think I need to know what they have planned for us. If the music is not an important part of it then, sadly, I think it has to go. You saw all those colours. Clothes, night-time lights, animals, nature. I would be kidding myself if I thought I could isolate myself from it. Knowing something was there and not being part of it; like living half a life. But the music may be crucial to our future. Do you mind if I ask Mac to join us?"

He pressed the call device and Mac arrived almost as if he had been waiting outside. Were we still under surveillance? Surely not, why would it be necessary?

"I need to ask you about my music." Mac nodded for me to continue. "You and the others obviously have a specific task in mind for us. If I keep my music gift will it be……?" I paused, "Will it be a help or hindrance?" This basic phraseology sounded more like Andrew than me.

"I have hinted about your future. The challenges

ahead of you. Nothing musical is involved and you will need to travel everywhere and meet many people. I believe it would make things more difficult for you. Answered simply, a hindrance. I know this sounds cruel and that it's something very personal and precious to you and I hesitate to destroy it, but there is another way. I can transfer it, so it will be kept alive and eventually enjoyed by many."

"Then, that is what I have to do. There's no sense doing anything half-heartedly. There will be other sacrifices, never to see Mars again or our Mothers.'" Something suddenly occurred to me. "Earlier you said the operations could be done simultaneously. Does that mean there is someone on this ship who would be the recipient? That all sounds so clinical, but you know what I mean."

"If there was, whom would you like it to be?"

"Certainly not Delman! Sorry, shouldn't be so venomous, but he's such a creep. I never really had much to do with the twins, and those weird conversations were so off-putting. Wesley I quite liked, he might be OK. But I think the best person would be Catalina. She has a caring nature and showed concern when the twins went missing. If she hadn't been so involved with the Monopoly, I think we would have become friends. And she has red hair like me! Though her eyes are blue, mine are green, like my Mum's."

"It seems you are a good judge of character, which will be useful later. Yes, Catalina is the one I had in mind. She has good musical abilities too; she sight reads music and has played the piano left handed since she was five. She now has full use of both hands and is practising scales as we speak. I think she will be a very willing recipient. Not that she will know anything about it until she is slowly introduced to colour. Her brain will assume that she's always had this ability and, with necessary adjustments, her family and friends will all believe the same."

"The wonders of modern science!" Andrew's barbed comment, he turned to me. "Jay, are you absolutely sure about this? It's so much part of you. I can help you through difficult situations. I can be your colour eyes in a colourless world."

"That's so lovely of you. Thank you but no, I'm sure this is the right way to go. Catalina sounds perfect. Would I be allowed to talk to her about it?"

"For security reasons, no. You will not meet again. I'm sorry, but that is how it must be. I will perform the operation myself, clandestinely, later tonight. There is another aspect to be considered, your clones. Can I take it you both agree to their activation?"

"Yes," we chorused.

"Then it will be necessary to make copies of your childhood memories, replicate your brain so they can become you! You have no reason to be frightened or worry about this, I promise you. Neither of you will be conscious when you are in theatre. Androids will assist and also collect you from your cabins at the appointed time. Afterwards they can be silenced with minor adjustments to their very limited positronic brains."

"It's been a long day. I'd like you to try and relax this evening. There is a whole new exciting world ahead of you. Tomorrow is your last day on this ship, and mine as I shall accompany you on the USS Endeavour."

Not sure what I think about that prospect.

After he'd gone we watched part of the earth film again, then got bored so picked up on the one we'd started yesterday. My brain was so full of this extraordinary, tough assignment. I was anxious too about loosing my colour music and couldn't stop thinking about the planned operation tonight. How much would I miss it? Would it be like cutting off my arm?

11

New names and afternoon tea

Thursday May 24th 2265

Morning

It was a strange night, although I can't say that I remember much about it. I'd lain awake for ages going over the day's events. Wondering what it would be like looking at that film again in silence. It was a different, odd, empty feeling and yet there was an excitement too.

I tried to write it all down but gave up as I became very emotional and miserable; ended up crying myself to sleep, something I haven't done since my grandparents left to return to Earth. Thinking about them made everything worse, they probably ended up on this ship, as I was five at the time; ie, post the V machine. I could not bring myself to say that horrible word, not even in my mind.

I was wakened at one am, by the two female androids. They were very kind and gentle and one asked me if I would please drink the sedative she held out. I was taken then to the Medical Centre where Mac was waiting. From then on I remember nothing until waking up just before eight. The same android was with me, sitting beside the bed. She spoke to me, almost whispering and clearly I heard her ask me how I felt and would I like a visitor?

A second or so later a very noisy Andrew arrived. I shushed him with my finger to my lips and begged him talk quietly.

"Hello," he repeated, "how do you feel?"

A knock on the door hailed the a rival of Mac. He smiled and asked me the same question. The android had gone.

"My hearing is so clear! All the fuzziness has gone and I think I could hear the tinniest sound; a piece of paper falling to the floor! Oh, Mac, this is unbelievable. I never thought about this positive aspect of the operation, I could only focus on the loss. How is Catalina? Does she know yet? Will she be able to cope and manage her new gift? This is a whole new world for her, and me. Sorry to be so emotional it's so overwhelming!"

"To begin with your hearing will be ultra sensitive. Andrew, you must remember to whisper. By the end of today it will be easier; for you both."

An android arrived with our breakfast pills and some more water; I was extremely thirsty and drank two glasses. "The anaesthetic," explained Mac. "Water will help flush it through your system; another glassful would be good. Stay here half an hour and then get dressed. Andrew and I will leave you in peace."

So I picked up my e-Tec meaning to continue what I'd started to write last night. I thought how nice it was to be quiet and not to have to talk to anyone, not even Andrew, although I resented that he'd been carted off before we'd even said two words to one another. Then I remembered our clones. What would they be like? Wesley? I expect so, they would be very 'new' and need 'socialising' as Mac put it. My mind wandered over to Catalina. I closed my eyes and could visualise her at her piano, dexterously running through her scales. I hoped she would be happy. I must have fallen asleep.

Andrew was sitting beside me when I woke up. "Hello, sleepyhead." he smiled, "it's nearly noon."

"How long have you been sitting there?"

"Oh, ten minutes or so."

I knew he was lying. It was that too casual voice of his, but I didn't mind, it didn't matter. "Is Mac waiting for us," I asked. "What have you been doing all morning?"

"Chatted to Mac a bit, nothing new or important. Then watched the film we saw the other night – not the one in colour about Earth, I thought we'd see that together later. Mac said to go over at one, by the way, no hurry. I say, if you're up to it we could see the Earth film now."

"I'd like that. Go and get it ready and I'll see you in five, although it may be ten," I said with a grin.

This time we saw the film right through. It was all so colourful and different. It's difficult to explain my feelings as I watched the approach to earth again, but without the music. I was sad to lose my gift, but also in a strange way a little bit relieved. I could enjoy the colours. The lions and elephants look so wonderful in their natural surroundings. The narrow streets in India, with ladies in their beautiful, bright coverings. I wondered if Mac would watch the film with us, then he could explain about their clothes.

I can see why free passage between the two planets is not allowed; no-one would ever want to return to Mars. The population majority are permanently here but there are a few, scientists and VIPs who go between the two. Hence the shuttle craft, which reminded me that we shall have to collect our stuff together soon.

"Well, Jay, what's it like to see colour in silence for the first time?" Andrew had been sitting patiently waiting for me to say something.

"Kind of sad, but exciting too. I'll get used to it. Earth looks a brilliant place! We have so much to look forward to. Live for the future."

I did a quick diary update as I was sure today would be a long one and didn't want to leave out anything.

Afternoon

As requested we joined Mac at one. A brief conversation about my health and we all sat down as usual.

"How is Catalina? I fell asleep dreaming about her playing the piano. Do you think she will play colour music?"

"She is already trying to do so, left handed, and at a very simple level. We have to remember that her right hand is only just learning to play! It will take time, but I am certain she is happy and content. Your clones have all your childhood memories and are still in the very early stages of development. They are kept separate for the time being, though, of course they may become friends later."

"But today is all about you, your new selves. We must establish whole new identities for you. The basis is formed, your family history and that side of things is fairly complete. We now need to go ahead with the formal documents, Birth and Health Certificates and National Registration numbers. These are not world-wide for obvious reasons. As your origin's are British, we thought we'd keep to that. The first thing for you to do is choose a name – your old ones will stay with your clones."

With his usual instant reaction Andrew immediately said, "John!"

"What do you mean, John?" I frowned. "You can't just say the first name that comes into your head. You'll have to live with this for the rest of your life!"

"Look, Jay, there's no point in messing about. John is a perfectly good name. It's short, to the point and insignificant! It will do fine." Then he asked, "Do we need a family name, too or will we keep our own?"

"Your family names are not unusual on Earth. We decided it would be easier to keep them and change your first names. Actually it was me that insisted on this. It could have been the other way around but there aren't too many Ophelia's in the world, and I sensed that Jay would agree."

He turned to me and I smiled gratefully back. "Do I have to decide now? It's such a big thing. To be named for one of my heroes would be good; Emmeline, Rosa, Amelia, Elizabeth, there are so many of them and so many names to choose from. But maybe they would be old-fashioned! I have no idea what names are acceptable on Earth. If, as you say, we are destined for great things then it must be a name fitting for the task………."

"Jay, you do not need to decide now, this minute. Any time today will do. But once decided then that will be final; you understand, John?"

Andrew looked momentarily bewildered, then grinned and said,"Aye, aye Captain!"

"How did you get on with the film today?" The question was for me this time.

"I thought it would be a good idea if we watched it with you. Maybe only extracts, like the scenes in India. All those brilliant people in strange clothes; a dazzling display of colour…..."

"Saris."

"The scenes with the huge trees with enormous leaves in so many shades of green and…...Sorry, Mac, what did you say?"

"Saris. The ladies were wearing a wrap-around garment called a sari. I have the film here, we can take some time to go through it."

It did take a while, but afterwards I felt I knew a bit more about Earth. Mac's film was longer, it included classroom scenes and children playing. There was also sport and part of a game where men were kicking a ball on a field with markings on. Football he called it. Then we saw people running and jumping and riding horses and sliding on a shiny surface with special shoes; that was ice skating. There was so much to see and take in. How will we ever remember it all.

Mac was very good and patient, stopping the film frequently to explain, answering our questions. I realised my attitude towards him was changing. Had he won my confidence, or was it simply that if we didn't trust him, there was nobody? Who was I to be now? Amanda, Angelina, Ann, Annabel? Barbara, Beth, Briony, Bonnie? Caroline, Cressida, Carmen, Christina? Diana, Dorothy, Delina? Emily,   Eleanor?,   I was working my way through the alphabet, completely oblivious to the others. It was such an enormous decision.

"What do you think, Jay?"

I turned to Andrew. "See. Completely out of it! Thought so. Mac wants to try us out on food – you know, that stuff you've seen in the photograph you told me about? Shall we have a go?"

I looked over at the other table. "It's called 'Afternoon Tea,'" Mac explained, "I thought we'd celebrate our British heritage. This is Victoria Sponge. It is not replicated but kept frozen since my last trip to Earth. It is easily digestible and I think you will like it. The red in the middle is strawberry jam. Oh, and this is tea. You may add milk or sugar if you wish – taste it first, it's very hot!"

This 'sponge' was light brown coloured with a dusting of white on top. When cut into, the inside was more yellow with a different texture. I broke off a small piece and nibbled gingerly at it. It was sweeter than I expected, especially the red bit, but I liked it. By the time I was ready for my second bite, Andrew had finished his. I think he is going to like this new feeding experience. The tea I didn't like until I added some of the ivory coloured milk. Great improvement, then I put a spoonful of sugar in too, immediately regretting it. Mac saw my expression and poured me another cup. I smiled at him, gratefully.

Andrew, who had finished his second portion of sponge, enthusiastically drank my sweetened tea, too. "Do you have this every day?" He asked.

"The drink, yes. The cake not so often. 'Afternoon Tea,' as a meal is an anachronism, but one in which I like to indulge occasionally. It would have been a daily occurrence in the first half of the twentieth century and before, particularly in the UK and the old British colonies. But this delightful meal was gradually abandoned, becoming quaint and outdated by the end of the century."

Andrew was full of enthusiasm, "I vote we resurrect it!"

But I was on a different track. "Mac, you said it wasn't replicated. What did you mean?"

"On the Endeavour all your food will be replicated. The taste and texture will be very similar to the original item on Earth, but will not be made from the same ingredients. You will be obliged to have lessons in cookery, so much of the time only the raw basic items will be replicated for you to be turned into something else. It is essential that you learn to cook. You cannot live on pills on Earth."

"You mean this sponge was made from different things mixed together? Will we learn to do this?" Andrew was interested now. "Sounds fun. A bit like chemistry."

"You will have help and there will be the finished items for you to taste, so you'll know what you're aiming at. But it is an acquired skill, which some people enjoy more than others. A whole new aspect of learning."

"I've just thought of something else." I'd really taken to Andrew's idea of thinking sideways, though, maybe this was only thinking round the issue. "For the past eighteen years we have eaten nothing but pills. How will our bodies react to all this new food?"

"That little problem was remedied last night. I

should have informed you earlier that your digestive system would need minor adjustments, and I apologise for omitting to do so. The procedure was simple, a mere formality, and you could not live on Earth without it."

I was not sure about this. My body was my body and *nobody* had the right to interfere with it unless I agreed. Had anything else about me been adjusted? *Slightly* altered? My original feelings of mistrust were aroused, and I wanted to talk to Andrew. We'd had almost no time on our own since Tuesday. Was this deliberate on Mac's part to keep us from discussing things? Even changing our mind's? Though how could we do that when our clones have stolen our identities? Suddenly everything was moving too fast – my whole world had changed. I needed to think, and not here.

"Jay? Jay, you've gone very pale," Andrew was peering at me. "You all right?"

I seized the moment, "No, not really. If you don't mind Mac, I'd like to lie down for a bit. Andrew, will you take me to my cabin?" There! I'd done it. Asserted myself as Mac is always telling me to do.

"What's up, Jay?" Andrew signed as soon as we were outside the door. He knew something was wrong and had the sense not to say out loud. "Have you had one of your feelings again? Or maybe the cake didn't agree with you!"

When we reached my cabin I sat on the bed. I asked Andrew if he trusted Mac. That certainly got his attention.

"What do you mean, trust him? Who else can we trust?"

Sulkily, I said out loud, "Maybe I'm being paranoid. I don't like being manipulated, that's all. I suddenly felt as if I wasn't in control of my own life. That digestion operation, however minor or necessary infuriated me! Are we out of our depth, Andrew? Are we being stupid? Should we be doing this?"

"I think I see what you're getting at. It's all happening so quickly and yet we're still here and nothing has happened! - I'm beginning to sound like you now! Not that I mean that nastily......."

"Andrew, shut up!"

"Yes, Ma'am," he replied laughing. "Come on, Jay. We'll be OK. Think of it as an enormous adventure, a special mission. The worst that can happen is that we hate living on Earth, but it's a huge place, not like Newton-Aldrin. If we don't like living in one city we can move to another! Even to another country. There doesn't seem to be much of a language barrier, English is universal now. Cheer up, Jay, be positive, we'll be fine!"

We sat talking about things. I also squeezed in a quick diary update. I don't know how long we were there, an hour, maybe longer, but it was nice to be on our own. To be able to discuss what we wanted without fear of judgement or being overheard. At least we presumed the surveillance had stopped, if it hadn't Mac was in for a few home-truths! And you know what? I didn't care!

One thing I did, was to pick up my e-Tec and take it through to the bathroom, just in case we were still being watched. I then checked that my diary was still there and changed the access code for one which I thought I would have been able to trace but no-one else could. I'd had an idea, a tiny inkling buzzing through my brain. I'd tell Andrew later. I copied the diary onto a minute Mem-Tic, tucking it into a special, secret hiding place within the old, tatty cover. I ensured it was completely concealed, replacing the e-Tec, and then joined Andrew.

"Have you thought of a name?" He asked as I returned from the bathroom.

"Haven't had much chance to, have I? Mac could have told us yesterday, given us more time."

"I didn't need time!"

"I know, but I do! It's a difficult proposition. Everyone hates the name their parents gave them, but finding another is different entirely."

"Perhaps I can help. Is there any name that you've always liked? What about your heroes idea?"

"What I need is a name that is fairly common but not boring. I'm so sick of avoiding Ophelia. I quite like the name Caroline but it's a bit long and everyone will call me Carrie or Carol."

"How about Carli?" Andrew suggested.

I thought for a moment and then said, "I like that! Carli, yes. Carli Meredith!" It had suddenly come to me. "I like it. The names roll off the tongue and go together well. And would suit a person who had a spectacular future! Thank you Andrew, you're so right. The only way is forward and there's no sense in being glum about it. Let's return to Mac and tell him who I am!"

I left the e-Tec by my bed before we left the room.

Mac was waiting for us. "I hope you have recovered Jay, you look a lot brighter, anyway."

"Yes, thank you, I am fine now. I've also decided on my new name; Carli, Carli Meredith. I hope that's OK?"

89

"Of course, and I think it's a very pretty name; it suits you. Well now, before it gets too late in the day I will set things in motion for your required paperwork. It'll take me a few minutes and while I'm doing it I have something for you." He handed a small pile of clothing to each of us. "I need you to change into these please. I'm sure you'll be glad to leave behind the conventional white uniform and wear something different. Everything is there for you including underwear. Your old clothes will be used by your clones – even your shoes. You should have no problems with this basic teenage attire, jeans, tee shirts with sneakers for your feet. You will be leaving everything else behind except your e-Tec, Jay, for obvious reasons, that will go with you. I have an identical one here to be left in your cabin."

"Now if you go along and change, I'll get on with this."

"Shall I take the new e-Tec with me? I'll need to leave it in my old cover otherwise Mum will think it odd."

"No, just bring the old one back with you, and I'll switch them over."

So, I thought, you don't trust me any more than I trust you! I felt like a ten year old being told what to do, however I didn't react as I was pretty certain he would not find the tiny hidden device. Maybe I could make the changeover myself under his scrutiny. Even if it was never found I had to leave it, just in case.

The new clothes were very different. The underwear was stretchy and cool and felt very comfortable, made from a different fabric from the usual cotton. The bra and knickers were obviously a set, in the same cream colour, with some lovely fancy edging. (I asked Mac later and he said it was embroidered lace.)The jeans weren't loose. They were stretchy, almost skin tight and showed off my shape. I stood on a chair and admired myself in the mirror, something that I'd never done before. With shapeless baggy uniform, who cared?

The tee shirt had a swirling orange and green pattern on, with splodges of yellow and electric blue. I was surprised how different I looked, and then and there decided never again to wear white. These colours enhanced my appearance.

I untied my hair leaving the band on the side in the bathroom and shook my head, hair falling over my shoulders in soft curls. I felt so different, so grown up! I wondered what Andrew would say. Then I thought, no, not Andrew, John, and I am the new Carli!

I picked up the e-Tec and my reader, not knowing whether I was to leave this or not, and returned to Mac's office. I stood outside feeling a bit shy, but then shook myself, took a deep breath and opened the door. They both stared at me.

"Wow!" This was Andrew's reaction, staring wide eyed, his mouth open, looking comical.

Mac smiled. "What a difference. You father chose all the clothes as they needed to merge in with general attire for your generation. I must say he did well on the colour."

Andrew – no, I must remember to say John – was wearing jeans also although his were not so tight and his tee shirt was a plain pale blue. It went with his dark, almost black hair and soft blue eyes. For the first time I thought he was handsome.

We sat and chatted for a while about our new clothes. Mac then produced two packages which contained my new e-Tec with it's own new cover. I held my breath as he swapped the devices over, putting the new one into my friendly old cover, transferring everything on to it. He'd inspected the old cover but hadn't spotted the tiny hiding place or the minute chip; I breathed a sigh of relief. Then he asked me to access my diary and deleted the entries from the end of April.

"Naturally I must remove your recent diary from the transferred data. You may keep it on your old one. One day it may make amusing reading."

How I didn't explode and sock him one I will never know. The condescension of the man! Had he been through all my personal information and read my innermost thoughts? I took a deep breath and forced my mouth into what I hoped was a smile but was probably more of a grimace.

"Yes. When I'm old and grey I'll read it to my grandchildren!" And then, flippantly. "What d'you want us to do now, then?"

Was Mac shocked by my reaction? I neither knew nor cared. He merely handed me back my e-Tec, with it's horrible new red cover.

"Perhaps you'd like to relax in the lounge for an hour. Your cabins have been cleaned and locked. You can keep your reader, there is another here for your clone, which has all the same books on. Return at six and we will have dinner together."

No thank you very much, I thought, as we left the room. I've had about enough of you for today. But I knew it was useless and I'd have to give in. I wondered what surprise he had in store for us next.

92

"You're in a strop." It was a statement, not a question. Andrew was looking enquiringly at me. - I must remember to call him John, but at the moment I just wanted Andrew, my old friend back again.

"Come on, tell me."

"The cheek of the man! The arrogance! That patronising, condescending attitude towards my writing, as though it's nothing, a childish whim! I hate him! And I'm sure he's been through everything; all my personal stuff, even my book collection. Is there nothing on this dratted ship that's private? Every time I think he's OK, begin to trust him, he goes and does something infuriating!" I was hopping mad.

"Have you thought it may be intentional? You know, bring out your aggressive side; prepare you for battle, so to speak?" He was all calm and collected. Usually it was him who lost his temper and me being cool, but the idea made me think. "You are rather gorgeous when you're mad!" He added with a wicked smile.

"I guess he could be winding me up. I never thought of that." I was calmer now and deliberately ignored his last remark.

"How about a game of chess for old time's sake, our last on this ship?"

A good idea but I wasn't in the mood and he won in record time. I couldn't concentrate. My thoughts were on Mac and what his next affront would be. I didn't have long to wait.

12

USS Endeavour

Evening

Thursday May 24th 2265

Just before six Mac walked into the lounge. "Time for you to have your first proper meal," he announced. "Come with me."

We followed like sheep; not to his quarters but through the other, originally locked doors to the floor below. We entered a small reception room and passed through a couple of doors, and along a short corridor which lead to a transfer bay. Here we were ushered into a small personal travel craft for a short journey to what I presumed would be the main shuttle.

When we landed the door was opened by a tall slim man with dark hair greying at the temples and clear blue eyes. He looked old, well, in his forties at least and had a vague familiarity about him. I was considering this when Andrew burst out, "What the hell are *you* doing here?"

"And a good evening to you too!"

"I might have guessed! You're as thick as thieves!" He turned to Mac, "Is the other one here, too?"

I was curious, but kept quiet, waiting.

"Are you going to do the honours, or am I?" Mac

said to Andrew.

"Jay, *this* is my father!"

Yes, of course, the resemblance was there. So this was the man who'd developed the killing machine. How can you live with yourself? I think Andrew interpreted my silence correctly and, from his expression, was thinking the same.

"I am delighted to meet you, Jay. I've heard a lot about you from Mac."

"Hello." We shook hands; "All bad, I have no doubt?" I added, coldly.

"Now why should you assume that? I think you've quite impressed him." Otto was smiling, or was it smirking, at me. I tried hard to return it but couldn't manage. My thoughts towards this man were so negative and I had no inclination to make small talk with him. But he was Andrew's father, and I felt guilty about hating him on sight because of the V machine. My mind wandered to my grandparents and I suddenly burst into tears.

Andrew put his arm round me and Mac produced tissues which I reluctantly took, mopped my tears and noisily blew my nose.

"Sorry," I sniffed. "It's been a long day, so much has happened, I really don't know who I am any more."

"Ah, yes, I must remind you that you are no longer Jay, but Carli. And Andrew, please start thinking of yourself as John. There must be no mistakes on the Endeavour, this is important to remember." Mac was looking sternly at us – like the school Headmaster when you've been sent to his study. It even felt the same; I was very much put in my place. "So, John, Carli, follow me."

We were taken through to the shuttle's main deck. It was not big, seats for a dozen or so, but we were the only passengers. I was offered refreshments by what I'm sure was an android, but, as I hadn't a clue what anything was, I declined.

Mac ordered 'fruit juice' for us and a drink for himself and Otto which I think he said was beer. It was a pale gold colour with a lighter coloured froth on the top; the fruit juice was pinky orange and tasted very nice. I asked what fruit it was, and was told it was a mixture – very helpful.

Andrew was looking accusingly at his father. "So, I'm still waiting to know what you're doing here?" Then, "How's Mum? I think it's appalling of you to deceive her. She must be out of her mind with worry. How can you live a lie?"

"Your mother is very well. She has become very engrossed with her work and has being doing some amazing research. She will be delighted to have you back with her again, fit and healthy."

"Having never been ill in the first place. How can you pull such an evil stunt?"

"Andrew, er, John, the important thing you must remember is to let go. Your mother will be fine and she will not remember anything about the reason you have been away for three months. Your replacement will be identical to you."

"Huh! Mind altering again are we?" Andrew was very unforgiving, and I could relate to everything he was saying. But I knew we had to be sensible. The past and our lives on Mars were over. We must leave that to our clones. He'd said it earlier – the only way is forward. I gave his hand a squeeze and while Mac was talking to Otto, signed quickly, it'll be all right.

"You still haven't said why you're here." Being Andrew, no, John, I must try to get it right, he couldn't let it go. He always wanted answers. Could it be that the man simply wanted to say a final goodbye to his son?

"The Universal Council have requested my presence, so I shall be travelling on the Endeavour with you."

Another bombshell! Oh, no, no, no. This news was awful. My dislike of the man was totally irrational but totally complete. I caught Andrew's eye; he was dismayed, too.

"How long will the trip take?" I asked.

"Less than an hour, so not long now. We're travelling at full speed. No need to keep the Endeavour waiting for longer than necessary," Mac replied.

"No," I responded irritably, "not this trip the one on the Endeavour?"

"That depends," Mac replied, "on when you are ready to live on Earth."

"But surely this is a routine trip. The Endeavour is only going to Earth isn't she?" Andrew was as fed up with the prospect of Otto as I was.

It was he who answered. "Mac, I think what John's getting at is how long he and I will be together on the star ship?" Otto turned to his son. "There are approximately eight hundred people on board. We can keep our distance if that is what you would prefer."

So that's where Andr... John gets his bluntness from! You know, I almost warmed to him for saying that. Maybe the ice would melt and we could be.... not friends exactly but rub along together civilly.

"I wonder, Mac if we shouldn't cast a little light on the matter of our plans? You have explained some of the background, maybe things would be easier between us if we are more explicit."

"I think not." Mac was obviously in charge. "It will wait until tomorrow. We shall be docking in about ten minutes and I expect the children would like to freshen up. The bathroom is at the rear of the craft."

Children! He'd done it again! I stomped off to the bathroom, Andrew in quick pursuit.

"Calm down, J…. Carli – hey, you know it's the first time I've called you that. He's only winding you up. You can see it's deliberate. Don't let him win! I'm glad Dad understood about us wanting privacy. He's quite good at picking up on hints, he has to be with Mum."

I looked at him and smiled, calmer now. "Yes, you're right. I can see it now. You know, we know nothing about each other."

"Other than I've got a brain as big as a planet and come from Mars!"

"Oh Andrew….."He gave me his raised eyebrow look. "Yes, I know but it's difficult I still think of you as Andrew – I probably always will. OK, John then. Please don't ever lose your sense of humour." I paused, "What I was going to say was that we need to spend some time getting to know one another, our families and childhood. I don't even know if you've got any brothers or sisters."

In typical Andrew fashion he came out with a stream of answers in one breath. "None, just me. Disruptive at school, totally bored, put up two grades. Good at numbers. No friends. Parents bickering, Dad

98

often away. That's about it really."

"That's not exactly what I meant," I laughed, "but it will have to do for now. Thank you for making me understand. I suppose we'd better go back." I looked in the mirror, "You know, I don't even have a hairbrush! We left everything behind. I hope Mac's thought of all this."

I would like to have known what the others were talking about while we were gone. I should have realised Mac was wanting rid of us. Oh to be a fly on the wall! I couldn't even lip read as they had their backs to us.

The android approached and told us to fasten seatbelts as we would soon be landing, so we did. We sat silently waiting to dock.

This landing bay was much bigger than the one aboard the Temeraire. I assume the smaller one we'd used when we left was only for crew as we'd originally boarded via a different area. There were other shuttles parked here and we walked passed them to the exit and stepped into the autolift. Wow, did it go fast! This ship must be enormous, I thought, looking at the list of levels.

We walked out into a beautiful sitting area. It was like the observation lounge on the other ship but much more luxurious. Several people sat at tables with drinks in front of them. Most wore obvious uniform with rank markings on their sleeves or shoulders. There were a few civilians. As we walked in a tall, ginger haired man stood and approached us. He had a nice smile and soft gentle eyes. Something about him was familiar, but, distracted, I dismissed it as I looked through the wide expanse of window, captivated by the view; it was so beautiful. I could see an amazing nebular of blue–green light shining in the distance.

Andrew nudged me. The man was speaking to me. "Hello, Ophelia!"

I went rigid, stared at him and then closed my eyes. No, this wasn't happening. Only one person called me Ophelia. I turned to Mac. "I'd like to go to my cabin now, please. Now, please," I repeated.

He hesitated, nodded and called over one of the stewards. "Can you take these young people to cabins 513 and 515, please?" He looked furious for some reason, but not with me. Maybe he understood more than I gave him credit for.

The cabins were much nicer than our old ones. A similar layout with separate sitting and sleeping areas and of course bathroom facilities, but very much more .... luxurious wasn't the right word. Mine was very feminine and someone had put flowers in a very pretty arrangement on my dressing table, they had a wonderful smell. Other things were there too. Hairbrush and a comb and some bottles of liquid with a strange nozzle on the top, which I pressed and a lovely scent filled the room. There two clasps. I'd seen these in films and was fairly sure they were for my hair. Other bits and pieces, too.

I was going through the drawers almost as an automaton, not taking anything in, when there was a knock on the door. I froze. Mac called out so I let him in.

"I am so sorry about that. I did not know that James was planning to be here tonight, otherwise I should not have taken you to the observation area. We should have been meeting him in three or four weeks time. Please accept my apology. If you and John want to stay and have your dinner here that's fine by me. I can have something sent."

Andrew was standing in the doorway. "What do you think?" I asked him.

"Assuming that man is who I think he is, then I think you should decide, if that makes sense? Double jeopardy for us both. We could avoid the issue until tomorrow but I for one need a good night's sleep and I'm sure neither of us will be looking forward to a confrontation in the morning."

"I agree. 'Once more unto the breach, dear friends, once more!'" Andrew gave me an inquisitive, raised eyebrow look. "Shakespeare, Henry V; maybe there's something of my father in me after all."

"United we stand and all that," he responded, and grabbed my hand. "We can do this, Carli."

On the way back I decided to be very grown up and calm. It was only a meal, even if it was our first, what could possibly go wrong? As we entered the lounge my father came towards us.

"I'm sorry," he apologised. "That was very wrong of me. I understand you are now Carli. I must say you've grown into a very attractive young lady."

I wasn't sure if he was going to hug me, but I wasn't ready for that, so took a step back. With an unfamiliar nervousness, I returned his smile; he did have a certain endearing charm. I introduced Andrew as John and they formally shook hands, eyeing each other; almost sussing out the enemy.

"I like my new clothes," I said, "Thank you," and motioned my hand towards my top. It was the first thing that came into my head. "I have decided I shall never wear white again!"

"I admit to having help with that, and all the other clothes in your cabin. I hope you like those, too. There is someone who I would very much like you to meet." He looked away and nodded towards an attractive woman with long dark hair taken up in a clasp at the back of her head. She had dark eyes and a smile that lit up the whole of her face as she responded to his invitation, coming towards us. Now it was my turn to eye up the opposition I thought, mischievously. Of course there had to be a woman in his life. Mum had told me he was a terrible flirt. Some people you take to immediately, others grow on you and others, only get worse with sinking feelings of hatred. How did I feel towards this couple? Do I call him Dad, Father, James, even? I had lapsed into one of my daydreams and Andrew nudged me out of it as the woman came to me and kissed me on both cheeks. I had missed her name.

"I'm so sorry, I was miles away."

"You'll get used to that!" chipped in Andrew. "Always away with the fairies!"

"Oh, dear. I feel all embarrassed now."

"Please don't. I am Elise. Your father and I have been married for five years, and I am very much looking forward to getting to know you and hopefully becoming a friend."

Her openness seemed genuine and I knew I wanted to accept her offer. Mac had been accurate all those days ago when he said I was a good judge of character, I had a quick mind for evaluating people and was usually right. That's what worried me so much about my feelings towards Otto. If Andrew and I were destined to spend the rest of our lives together then this

102

man would surely have to be part of it.

In retrospect the evening went amazingly well. I think everyone was on their best behaviour and it made things easier. Andrew and I were advised to try something simple that would be easy to digest, and we both opted for the 'omelet with mashed potatoes and peas' that Elise suggested. Our first real meal. I don't know what I thought of it, I was too busy watching everyone and thinking of sensible things to say. It was better than those dreadful pill times before, but not much, if I'm honest. I was so nervous.

Dad or James, I haven't decided which yet, and Elise were the ones who held the conversation; jollying things along. They seem to be very sociable types. Mac and Otto were quiet. Andrew and I, sitting opposite each other, were able to sign, and Mac, seated at one end was unable to follow. Otto scowled at his son, disapproving. I suppose it was a bit rude to exclude the others, so I signed to say enough. Elise suggested we try crème caramel as a second course. Very nice. Andrew had a second portion. A couple of hours had passed with not a lot said of significance, I guess we were all being careful and thinking of what could wait until the morning.

It's now later and I am sat here in bed with my diary, wondering how my clone is getting on – probably not so different from Catalina as we last saw her. She was nice, I would have liked the chance to get to know her better; I hope she's enjoying her new gift. Maybe she and the new Jay will be friends. What about Jay and Andrew? Maybe their lives will all be entwined.

13

My new family

Friday May 25th 2265

I awoke to the sound of knocking and Elise asking if I was awake. Sleepily I called her in. She was dressed in black trousers that fitted well across her hips but fell loosely around her legs. Her crimson shirt flattered her. It was tucked into her trousers with a shiny, wide black belt. She looked very elegant. Her hair was piled on top of her head and fastened with a silver pin.

"I thought you might like some company. John is with his father in the dining room, eating croissants. I think Otto shooed him out of bed an hour ago. I hope you slept well. Did you find all your new clothes? My choice, I'm afraid, but as soon as we get to Earth you can go shopping and find your own."

"If they're like those I wore yesterday they will be fine. I love the underwear. I've never worn pretty clothes before, only Mars uniform. I haven't had much chance to see the other things."

Elise was opening wardrobe doors and showing me dresses and trousers and tops. They were so pretty and colourful. Tears pricked my eyes and rolled down my face. I was completely overwhelmed. She sat on the bed and hugged me.

"There is so much for you to see and do and discover.

I wasn't sure at first but now I'm so glad that James insisted on our being on the Endeavour to meet you. He called in a few favours to be here and we travelled on the Santa Maria from the USA, to rendezvous with her, having first flown from Paris……. Oops! I wasn't supposed to say we live in Paris. Not sure why but Mac's orders." She held her hand to her mouth in alarm.

But Mac had told us. "It was because of influencing Andr…. John and me when it comes to deciding where to live." I giggled. "I won't tell if you don't!"

Thus a simple bond was formed between us. Was it Mac who'd said, "Trust your instincts?"

It took a short while for me to shower and dress. I pulled on the same jeans, (I liked this skin tight image.) and teamed them with a plain purple top. Elise brushed my hair and pinned it back with the most gorgeous hair slide. Then we reported to the dining room. Outside she paused and said with a smile, "Now, don't let the boys bully you."

"Carli! You've overslept and missed all the croissants!"

"What you mean is that you've eaten them all!" I retorted to Andrew.

But then a voice behind me said,"Here you are. Coffee or hot chocolate and croissants." It was Otto. I was so taken aback and stared wide eyed at him. "They're not poisoned, you know," he said with a smile.

Good humouredly he set the plate and mugs in front of me. I still didn't know what to think, so just said, "Thank you." They were all looking at me. I took a small bite of a warm croissant, umm, and sipped first the chocolate – the word being familiar to me – then the coffee. The coffee was bitter, then James / Dad / Father passed the cream.

"Thank you." I hesitated and concentrating on him said, "I don't know what to call you." The tears were coming back and I blinked them away, but my eyes were still watery, so I blew my nose. Why, oh why, was I so emotional?

"I haven't been much of a father to you for the last fourteen years, so maybe James would be a good idea."

Inwardly I thanked him for his honesty. No, he hadn't. He'd walked out on Mum and me and I had hated him for it. She'd never told me why he'd left. Now I was confused. I didn't know how I felt towards him.

Andrew came to my rescue. "Your hair is nice like that, pinning it back keeps it out of your eyes." He looked at me with an expression that said, 'I hope I've said the right thing, I'm not very good with words.' Funny, I could read him like a book. It was almost a telepathy between us. Thinking back it had always been there. I must talk to him about it when we're on our own.

Mac, in his headmasterly fashion, took charge. "I suggest we have a rest day today, and tomorrow as well. It would be nice for the children to explore the ship."

There he goes again, I thought! Children!

"There are no restrictions, apart from the Bridge, of course. If you want to go to Engineering then you will need permission – I suggest you leave that until later. The first three levels are engineering and science labs. Then there are the cabins and private living accommodation from four through to eight. Nine and ten are the children's area, with schools, nursery and their various amenities.

We are on eleven and you will find the observation

106

lounge and other communal areas here. While I think of it, there is also a formal dining room. As it was Carli's eighteenth last Tuesday we all thought it would be nice to have a celebration dinner tonight. It will also mark a turning point for you both."

For the first time in my life I wondered what I should wear. It was an odd feeling – to be able to choose anything and look different again. How sad those living on Mars were, having only uniform, deprived of colour and being able to choose what they wanted to look like.

Mac was still talking; the Medical Centre and Environmental labs, and then he referred to 'Holodecks' on levels fifteen and sixteen. "Best that your first visit to these is accompanied; you'll need instruction on their use. You will be using their programs a lot as time progresses. Perhaps James and Elise would take you tomorrow?"

There he was again, organising everyone. He gave us a plan of the Endeavour, which Andrew glanced at dismissively, but I folded and put in my back pocket.

"If you'd like to join us at one then we can have lunch together in the Observation Lounge, which is generally known as Effie, officially Eleven Five. Off you go and enjoy yourselves."

Once more I felt like a child being sent out to play. I suppose it was just his manner, but that didn't mean I had to like it.

It was good to be on our own. Outside the door we waited and thought what to do. I think we'd both had enough of exploring spaceships for the time being. Together we looked up and said, "Your cabin or mine?" Then both laughed. Was there a telepathy between us?

We ended up in 515, Andrew's, (Oh heck! I must stop

calling him Andrew, even if it's only in my diary. I hereby promise not to write or say Andrew ever again!) having first gone to mine as on the Temeraire, but An….. John started sneezing because of the scented flowers. I wondered if Elise had put them there? I should have asked her earlier.

It was so nice sitting and chatting. We talked about our childhood and family traditions; likes and dislikes; school and favourite books and paintings. We could have been at the Newton-Aldrin art gallery at the same time as kids. There were some great paintings by the Old Masters and from the French Impressionist era and a lot by more modern twenty-first century painters. This was where I had first seen the name Temeraire, though Turner had painted her after her capture, when she had been stripped of anything useful, on her way to be scrapped; appearing almost like a ghost ship.

We thought we'd try out the telepathy idea. I told John to think of some random thing and concentrate on it. When a picture of me in my ugly white uniform came into my mind, I giggled and told him to stop messing about! We tested it again several times with different objects. Each time I was right. It was amazing! Then we tried the other way around. I started with the flowers, but that was a bit obvious, and he did guess it on the second try. Then I thought of the very pretty hair-slide I was wearing and he said, "Your dark red hair!" On the right line, I thought, so I switched to my e-Tec and he got that immediately. We carried on for a while and guessed correctly most of the time.

"You know this could be really useful. We need to practice, and with abstract things like feelings, too." Instantly I knew we both wanted to keep it secret.

A while later, John, (see, I'm getting better!) said he was thirsty. "I could do with a drink. Some of that fruit juice we had yesterday would be good."

I agreed, so we made our way to Effie in search of some. We sat by the window, looking out at the real stars this time; they were so beautiful. A steward was very helpful; identified what we wanted and brought it to us. He was the same one who had shown us to our cabins yesterday and he remembered us. He was open and friendly, treating us like honoured guests.

Half an hour later my heart sank as Otto approached our table, asking to join us. We couldn't very well say no so he sat down.

"From your expressions I know you don't want me here, but there is something that I need to tell you both. The people I work for, that is the Guardians, can be denied nothing. To be blunt, they rule the world. When I was ordered to develop the Vaporiser I did it under great duress. There was no alternative. Well, there was, if you consider banishment to the penal colony on Titan an option. If not me someone else would have done it. This invention was, and still is top secret. Believe me your abhorrence of it is nothing compared to mine. Since its inception I perceived its planned use and did my best to sabotage or destroy it but to no avail. This concept was illegally discussed with James and Mac and we decided that somehow the Guardians have to be stopped."

"I don't know how much Mac has told you, but this trip has been planned for sixteen years. We need you to tell the World what is happening here on Mars, with the elderly, the sick and the disabled. The Guardians want perfection and we have got to stop them. You must understand that this is the prototype for the future; for Earth."

"The question going through your minds when we met yesterday, was 'How can I live with myself?' The answer is simple, with enormous difficulty. Not being able to discuss my work with your mother," (this to John,) "is a tremendous strain and has told on our relationship. Mac and James have kept me sane. .... Now, enjoy your drink and I'll see you in half an hour for lunch – or not." He stood, nodded and left us, stunned.

John responded true to form. "Flipping heck!"

It is hard to write down exactly what I thought at that moment. The anger had gone and I almost felt sorry for him having to develop such a horrible machine, but there *must* have been other work he could have done. I still don't really like the man he's too abrupt, with no finesse, jumping straight in with both feet in his arrogance. Then I realised I had described John! I was getting used to his bluntness and idiosyncrasies. Should I wonder that his father was the same? I was feeling guilty about being so judgemental. I needed to give him a second chance. They say everyone deservers that, so maybe my father should have one, too.

We discussed his revelations; John's feelings were similar to mine, but in a different way. He'd lived with this man all his life and yet hadn't known him.

While we talked James and Elise arrived for lunch and we ordered new things from the menu. Elise introduced us to Ice Cream, I don't think John will ever eat anything else! He is totally captivated. You know, I am, too. Not with ice cream, although the chocolate variety was rather yummy, but with Elise. James, too

110

has an enormous amount of natural charm. I can understand what Elise sees in him. I wonder if he was like this with my mother. Why had they split up? Dare I ask him?

At exactly this moment James spoke to me. "Day dreaming again? What are you thinking about?"

And then, before I even realised, I was asking "Why did you leave us?"

The silence that followed was awful. I listened to my heart thumping away and I knew I shouldn't have asked. John thought so, too, but didn't say. It was Elise who broke it.

"Your mother has never said anything to you about it?" I shook my head. "Then, James I think you must be honest. Hopefully Carli is old enough to understand. You have been wanting her to know about Catalina. Now is as good a time as any. Would you prefer if John and I left you in private?"

"No!" I was emphatic. I'd rather John was here, then I wouldn't have to repeat it later. Elise obviously knew what was coming; it might be easier if she remained. I was intrigued now and also wondering what Catalina had to do with it. Today it seemed it was the day for enlightenment or confession, if that's what it was.

James took a deep breath. "Catalina is your half sister. I had an affair with her mother when you were a baby."

I let this revelation sink in, then exploded. "The only thing she told me was that you were a flirt! By flirt read womaniser! How could you be so disloyal? So? What then? She found out and threw you out? You abandoned us and them and fled to Earth?" I was in a foul temper and wasn't backing down.

I knew I shouldn't have asked. Catalina? I never expected this. I got up and ran towards the door almost crashing into our nice steward. As I glanced back, Andrew rose to follow me but was held back by Elise. I wanted to be alone, but was too upset to try and tell him telepathically.

When I reached 513 the tears came. Why was I suddenly a cry-baby? My emotions were all screwed up; I couldn't take any more. I sobbed and sobbed and eventually pulled myself together. Why am I upset? For my lost childhood? For my mother who I would never see again? For the sister who I hadn't even known about and never had the choice or the chance to get to know? Or just the way my so called father had destroyed my life?

I sat on the bed thinking about all this and more. Andrew, (no, John, I can't even get that right now!) knocked and put his head round the door.

"I couldn't wait any longer, but I'll go if you prefer."

"No, please stay. I'll probably shout at you, but it's not your fault. How could he? How can he be so cold hearted and unemotional about what he did?"

He listened to me for a long time. Not saying anything only being there, letting me rant. One thing he does understand is a good rant, I thought. And then almost as fast as it had blown up, my tantrum ceased.

"Wait here for a moment," he smiled. Less than five minutes later he was back with a mug of hot chocolate! It was exactly what I needed.

"Only one?" I enquired.

"No time, I just wanted to get back to you."

I thought about this and then compared him to his father. I suddenly wondered if Otto had ever sung

'Happy Birthday' standing on a bar table? Had he recited the periodic table or all those mathematical figures to someone special because he had nothing else to give them? Yes, Andrew had his father's bluntness and was a bit temperamental, but he had a heart of pure gold and I was so glad we had found each other.

We shared the drink and talked about Otto and James. Finally John said, "Elise asked me to find out if you wanted to have this celebration dinner tonight or not?"

"I don't know. What do you think?"

Unfair of me to ask him. He hesitated and then answered in his very 'matter of fact' voice.

"Yesterday's dinner went OK. But I think tonight's will be very strained unless you and James can talk first. How do you feel about that? They are probably still in Eleven Five if you can face it."

I considered the prospect and decided that the conversation would have to take place sooner or later. "Might as well get it over with."

Elise and John left us to it. My mood was more rational now, I could see things clearer and less emotionally. James started to tell me about his life with Mum and then everything since his arrival on Earth. I told him about my childhood on Mars and my writing. We were both remarkably frank and honest, leaving nothing wanting, no question unasked, except one. A movement in the corner of my eye caught my attention as John had been out-played by Elise on the chess table. Good on you, girlie, I thought, but then wondered if John had arranged it that way. He didn't lose very often, and he might have thought it appropriate.

He caught my thoughts and smiled. Then they came over and sat down. There had been no outbursts or shouting and both looked hopefully towards us.

Naughtily I asked, "I suppose I don't have any other unknown siblings, do I?"

It was Elise who answered, nervously. "Fabian and Xavier, twins. They are only four and are at home with my parents."

I should have expected this. I was shocked at first, but then delighted. I had a whole new family, two little brothers and a sister, even if I should never see her again. I was deep in thought when Elise showed me some photographs of two delightful bundles of mischief. They both had their mother's dark hair, but with blue eyes and captivating smiles. John looked over my shoulder in approval.

We spent the rest of the afternoon together. James and Elise had been aboard for a few days, so they took us up to the Holodecks and demonstrated a couple of the programs. It was amazing! I could have sworn everything was real. We were introduced to the few members of the crew we passed. One was from Engineering and John couldn't wait to ask if we could visit. I think we'll enjoy our time on the Endeavour, however long or short it may be.

14

Retail therapy!

Saturday, May 26th 2265

I slept well after the emotional upheaval of the day and awoke, very early, refreshed. Time for my diary and a little catching up on events.

Elise helped me dress last night. When she'd showed me the clothes earlier I hadn't really taken anything in, but later, I tried on all three dresses and decided on the emerald green one. It was a heavy, flowing fabric called jersey with a navy elastic belt, which had a fastening buckle with orange and green glittering stones in. She produced a similar necklace from one of the drawers; very pretty and very feminine. All these new words I must try to remember and use – a whole new language of fashion. Again she pinned my hair for me, sort of half up and half down, this time fastened with a plain gold clip. But best of all were the shiny gold strappy sandals with their two inch high heels! I liked these, they completed the outfit. However will I remember all these new words?

I wondered if John would need any help choosing what to wear, but was firmly told that Otto was organising him. Makes a change from Mac, I thought, meanly. I still didn't like or trust him. I don't even think I can say why, call it intuition. James had won me round, I admit that; he had an abundance of natural charisma. Even Otto had begun to grow on me; an older, harsher version of John. But Mac?

John was waiting for me outside my door. He wore a pale blue shirt, the colour of his eyes again, with darker blue trousers. I linked my arm through his and we made our way to the dining room. They embarrassed us by clapping and cheering as we entered, it was awful! I was showered with compliments – I'd already had the seal of approval from John, so I knew I looked OK.

I haven't said anything about the new food we were eating, except for the breakfast, of course. At this special meal everyone ordered something different and John and I got to taste it all. Oh, and we started with Champagne. Not genuine we were informed because of the no alcohol rules on board ship but Elise, who's origins are French if you haven't already guessed, said it wasn't too bad but that as soon as we arrived on Earth we would have the real McCoy. I asked who McCoy was and they all laughed, breaking the ice and setting the mood for the evening, which turned out to be most enjoyable.

At the end of the meal I saw Elise catch the attention of our steward, thinking nothing of it. A little while later he returned with a cake that was on fire! I was horrified! John made a dash towards the nearest fire extinguisher, but was held back by Otto. Elise took my hand and told me not to be afraid, this was a birthday cake and I was to blow out the candles and make a wish.

I did as I was told and called out, "A wish!" Not having a clue what I was meant to do. Again everyone laughed. The ritual was explained and the candles re-lit. I took a deep breath and extinguished them while they sang the 'Happy Birthday' song, but I can't tell you my wish or it won't come true.

Time is moving on and I suppose I should get showered and dressed. There are some tight black jeans in the drawer and I thought I would wear them today. Dare I wear a red top?

John left his cabin at the same time as I did so we arrived together for breakfast. Otto was there eating a bacon sandwich, and drinking tea. We ordered the same which we both liked. I was asked which tea I wanted and looked to Otto for help. We established that I'd had ordinary black tea with milk before, so that's what I was given.

Otto ordered toast so we shared that spreading strawberry jam, marmalade, honey and lemon curd from the various pots on the table. Collectively these are preserves and we tried a different one on each mouthful. How indulgent can we get? James and Elise arrived as we were finishing; they opted for coffee and croissants as yesterday.

"Do you have any plans for today?" Otto asked. I looked at John and we both thought no, not really.

"Do you have any suggestions, Dad? We haven't really thought about it yet."

"I bumped into Reg from engineering earlier and he was asking if you'd like to visit the engine room?"

It wasn't really my scene, but I could read John's enthusiasm. "I can always catch up on some reading," I said. "Go on, I'll be fine."

"I've a better idea than that;" this was Elise. "We could go shopping!"

"Shopping?"

"Yes. Of course we won't be able to buy anything as we'll be on the holodeck, but we can try things on and have a browse. Have a girlie morning."

I wasn't sure what I was agreeing to but it sounded fun, and we set off together when she had finished her breakfast.

There were many different programs and we, well Elise, chose one she called 'Harrods'. She said it was a world famous department store in London. She asked for the ladies clothing section, then changed her mind to 'teenage' wear. Wow! The whole place was full of the most amazing clothes. I tried on a whole heap of things and then persuaded her to transfer us to the ladies section so she could have fun, too.

"They do have some shops on board; level fourteen, I think. There are some bars and more places to eat as well. Why don't you and John go and have a look this afternoon?"

I pulled out my map. There was nowhere called 'shops.' Elise looked over my shoulder; "That's it! Deck Twelve not fourteen; labelled '*Retail*.'"

Our next destination was called 'The Food Hall' and we trawled through the most intriguing looking food area. All the time she was telling me about cheese and fruit and cakes and wine, all sorts of different things. She seemed to know what everything was called, and laughed when I told her how clever she was to know about it all.

"You'll get used to it. Gradually it will become second nature to you, as will cooking and food preparation."

Then I remembered something. "Do you know

118

what a Victoria Sponge is?"

"But of course. I make them at home quite often. I think Mac took one back with him on his last visit."

"Yes! He said it had come from Earth! Did you really make that? We had it for 'afternoon tea.' It was our first real food, last Thursday and was delicious. Is it very complicated to make? Could I learn, do you think?"

"Certainly! It is not difficult. I will teach you." She smiled, then turned towards me and gave me a hug; a real genuine hug of friendship and love.

We all met up for lunch; even Mac was there, wearing star ship uniform. (That of Commander I later found out.) He had been requested to take over from an injured officer who would be off sick for a while. Good, I thought, the less we see of him the better; now we only need to get rid of Otto!

As if he had heard my thoughts Otto announced that he would be helping an acquaintance in Engineering for a few days; he would, however, join us for dinner in the evenings.

Perfect, I thought, relieved. Oops! I mustn't look too happy. Nor must you John, as I picked up his relief, too.

"We could begin the schedule with Food and Cookery?" Elise suggested. "It is, after all, an important part of living on Earth."

"I was hoping you'd say that," agreed Mac. "You'll need to find appropriate programs but I've booked sixteen four for the rest of the week. If you and James make a start, then we'll take over soonest."

Not looking forward to that. Oh stop it brain! Stop being so negative! Was John thinking the same? I

119

couldn't tell. Suddenly the image of a Victoria sponge came into my head. So he'd remembered that, too. I grinned at him conspiratorially.

"We'll need to draw up a program and check ingredients and equipment, so we'll start in the morning. No, Monday would be better, you did say we were to have a couple of rest days." Elise smiled at me. I was sure Mac was about to argue, but he was silenced by a challenging stare from Elise. Hmm, I thought, who is really the boss? I remembered her saying not to let the boys bully me.

I told John all about Harrods, but he was elated by his engineering tour. This new ship is Galaxy class and travels at an amazing speed. The journey to Earth will only take us four weeks! I'm so excited, I can't wait to see it.

We enjoyed our afternoon on Retail. There were several shops specialising in different things. I headed for the clothes shops, of course, and, although he said he didn't mind these, he was noticeably embarrassed by the displays of ladies underwear and preferred the gadget shop with all sorts of electrical bits and pieces.

We wanted to try different fruit juices in a café called Romano's but realised we had no ability to pay for anything, so returned to Effie and found our friendly steward, who produced a variety of juices, saying they were on a special account- no payment required.

While we were there, James and Elise joined us, so we explained about the incident in the café. Understanding, James nodded, "We need to arrange allowances for you both. I'll sort it with the others."

There followed a discussion about the personal credit system. It seems pretty straightforward but I

120

think it'll take a bit of getting used to. We never bought anything on Mars as there were no shops and nothing to buy!

15

We meet an Australian

Sunday, May 27th 2265

I sat down to write my diary and almost decided not to! It wasn't that it was a rotten day, on the contrary, but there was nothing very significant about it and I don't want this to become boring, repetitive trivia, but here goes anyway.

It was fun visiting the other decks and finding out what goes on. We even met Mac in the Med Centre. He was talking to the officer he replaced, who seemed a very nice lady. We stayed and chatted to her after he had gone. She had an unusual accent and she told us she came from Australia and talked about Brisbane and said how hot it was there. Mac had previously told us not to tell anyone we were from Mars and it became difficult to think of things to say after a bit. Luckily she was called away for treatment so we left, returning to Romano's and spent our first credits on Cappuccino and a Danish, another suggestion from Elise.

Giving deck nine a miss as we'd both had enough of school, we found that ten was mostly physical education, with a gym and what we concluded were games areas with marked out courts and things. We'd played team games on Mars but didn't recognise any of the marked out areas.

Again we lunched with James and Elise and it was useful to talk things through with them. I asked what Commander Johnson meant by Brisbane being hot.

"Ah. Weather will be a totally new ball game for you."

John and I exchanged thought's. "We saw the marked courts on Ten. Do we play it there?" he asked. James explained.

We were still laughing when Mac came through the door, scowling.

"I'd like to know what you two were doing in the Medical Centre?"

Immediately on the defensive John's response was typical. "It wasn't the Bridge; not out of bounds!"

"Don't be smart with me! I don't want you gossiping to all and sundry! I forbid you to go there again. In future you James, Otto or myself will accompany you at all times!"

Speechless, John and I swapped telepathic insults. His language was becoming very ripe. Maybe it was the new books he was reading, not the censured editions from Mars.

Elise protested, but this time was shouted down by Mac. He went on and on about security and secrecy with regards to our defection. It occurred to both of us that we might end up being locked in our cabins, prisoners.

Mac didn't stay long. He didn't even stay for lunch, just yelled at us and left. I wondered why he had been in sick bay himself, but answered my own question – of course, he was a doctor. Maybe he needed to catch up with the officer he replaced?

"Don't worry," Elise looked sympathetic, "He'll

calm down and I'm sure we can work something out."

"What is 'weather?' you never got a chance to tell us."

James took over. "Atmospheric condition, climatology. It's on your tuition list. Something you have to experience to understand; sunshine, rain, wind, snow. We'll see what the programs have offer on sixteen four."

All these new words to remember. I must keep using them. But it's the colloquial phrases that James comes out with that are fun. Those little nuances that pepper the English language and make it what it is.

16

Making cakes

Monday, May 28th 2265

I made my first Victoria Sponge today!

It was an early start, we were outside sixteen four at eight o'clock, to appease Mac as much as anything. But, as he never turned up for breakfast, he wouldn't have known anyway.

Elise had prepared all sorts of ingredients. She thought it would be a good idea to make our lunch and then later cook dinner for everyone. John was devastated – we both were, and pleaded with her to show us how to make the sponge cake. With good humour she gave in and from another cupboard produced butter, sugar, flour and eggs and a small bottle of something she called vanilla essence. Then, as an afterthought, found a tin of cocoa.

She suggested we make different ones, so we could have them for tea later. I made the one we'd tasted before with strawberry jam in the middle and John added cocoa powder to make a chocolate version, with a chocolate cream topping, (mine had vanilla butter cream.) Under Elise's excellent tuition we managed quite well. Not as perfect as the one she had made, but she was very complimentary. It had taken all morning, what with the washing up and tiding away.

Otto arrived just as we were about to sit down to a cake lunch with some tea. He was with James and Mac arrived soon after. He appeared to be in a good mood, for once.

"I had a sneaking suspicion that lunch may be afternoon tea!" Mac took the proffered plate, containing a slice of each. "Not bad. For a first effort, not bad at all. Can I guess that you made the chocolate one?" He smiled at John, who had made no secret of his fondness of the confection and usually had some in his pocket 'for emergences.'

"Yes, well done both of you." Otto stood up, holding his mug. "More tea anyone?"

It was a happy occasion and Elise invited them all to dinner here in sixteen four. A challenge was set.

We both enjoyed cooking. John likened it to chemistry. He was chopping peppers for the pasta sauce when he cut his finger and screamed. Elise said it wasn't a big cut, but still took him (under protest because of Mac's threat), to sick bay, where they cleaned it up and miraculously repaired the cut. I went with them for the experience and to keep a look out for Mac. But he wasn't around and the Australian lady wasn't either.

There are no knives on Mars, at least I've never seen one, so, I suppose it was an accident waiting to happen. Neither of us had ever seen blood. Later, I had difficulties with my potato peeler, trying to peel, not potatoes but apples, for my pudding, but I didn't trust myself to use a knife as I certainly didn't want to end up in sick bay.

It was a lovely day, and we all enjoyed our dinner; spaghetti bolognese with apple crumble and custard to

126

follow. Elise was a good teacher. We even had a glass of wine. I wonder what we'll make tomorrow?

17

Chatting with Elise

Friday, June 1st 2265

We've spent all the week cooking in sixteen four with Elise. The others, mostly James, joined us for lunch and/or dinner. Even Mac came a couple of times. It was good to have their support with this new venture. We both had disasters with our dishes, though not on the same day thank goodness, and everyone was very understanding, even if we did end up using the replicator when my chicken dish was inedible. I think I'm better at puddings than main courses. I certainly prefer making them. Either that or I must get better at following recipes.

Elise and I were talking earlier today about her children and their life in Paris. "With four year old twins you must be kept pretty busy." I said, thoughtfully. She explained that they had a house robot who was great help with the little ones. "Otherwise I could not have left them with Maman and Papa for so long. They are in their fifties and the boys can be quite a handful sometimes. They are at pre-school from Monday to Friday, until lunch time. They are used to being with my parents and I have been able to call them every evening before they go to bed."

But I missed the last bit. I was sidetracked as

usual, away with the fairies, as John would put it. "You still call your father Papa?"

"I do."

"And what do the boys call James?"

"They call him Papa, of course. It is the French way of saying Dad or Daddy."

I though for a moment, unsure how to put this next question. An idea had been going round my brain for a few days now. "Elise. Do you think James would mind if I called him Papa? You see I've been thinking about this. He is my father even if I've only just found him, and somehow it doesn't seem right to call him James. After all there are many people I can call James but only one person in the world who could be Papa and somehow it seems more appropriate than Dad."

John had been washing up and clearing the kitchen. He paid no attention to us but I know he heard; I could sense it. I could also sense that he was pleased by the idea. He liked James and Elise, too.

"You are serious about this, aren't you?" She asked me.

"Yes. I've been thinking about it for a while. Do you think he would mind? Maybe you should ask him first? I don't want to be too forward or embarrass him or……."

"You won't, I'm sure he will be delighted. Perhaps on the first occasion, though, choose your time carefully. Maybe not in front of everyone else. It is, after all a very private thing between the two of you.

About five minutes later James popped his head around the door. "How's supper coming on, I'm starving?"

I took my cue from Elise as she vaguely nodded. I

smiled at him and said, "A few more minutes, Papa. Perhaps you would open the wine?"

I don't think I can justly describe the look on his face as my words took effect. He was obviously taken aback. He looked to me and then to Elise, who only smiled. For an awful moment I thought he was going to cry and I admit that tears were beginning to prick my eyes, too.

"Well, having lost the only parent I knew, it would make sense to acknowledge the one I have now if you see what I mean? Is it OK?"

But he didn't get a chance to answer as Otto and Mac turned up, noisily arguing about something, which turned out to be about what was on the menu for this evening.

This was our hardest meal so far. The idea had been Roast Beef and Yorkshire Pudding but getting everything ready and cooked for the same time proved to be a nightmare. At Elise's suggestion we cheated and replicated the Yorkshire Pudding at the last moment. John's roast potatoes were yummy. I suddenly remembered the photograph of my mother's; this was what the pile of golden brownish things were.

I liked these meal times when we all talked about our day. Mac announced that we would be doing different things next week. He was no longer required for duty and would go through our 'training course' with us in the morning.

John, I thought, as he reacted to this statement, you can tell me later what that phrase means! He grinned and I caught Mac observing us, with an odd expression. Oh heck, I thought, please don't let him be telepathic too!

130

18

Weather

Saturday, June 2nd 2265

Apparently they have two rest days on Earth, Saturday and Sunday, though, of course a lot of people have to work shifts rather than the basic week. Anyone in retail or medicine, for example would have two different days off. I asked why Sundays and was met with an odd silence.

I should have said this was Saturday morning and we were having breakfast, later than usual, and chatting afterwards.

"Religion," was Mac's short reply. He looked at Papa. "I believe you're down for that."

When we were with everyone I still sometimes thought of him as James, probably because Mac was so bossy, but he was openly Papa now.

"Sex, drugs and rock and roll." James was being flippant, Mac scowled at him, Otto sniggered, Elise looked down and we sat there wondering what the fuss was.

"Weather!" Mac exclaimed. "We'll begin today. Fifteen two is booked from ten and there are several helpful programs readily available."

"I thought Saturday was a rest day," John protested.

Mac was insistent. "Weather needs to be experienced, not like lessons at all. You can go for a walk in the park!"

I picked up John's indignant thoughts. "Language," I said out loud to him. Oops, stupid mistake, but luckily no-one seemed to have noticed. I didn't blame him, I was pretty fed up as well. We'd made plans for today, which would now have to wait.

"Don't forget to take thick coats with you," he continued. You'll find several in the wardrobes on sixteen. James, you and Elise will accompany them. Otto can fill you in later on the theory."

Dismissed, we dutifully reported to deck fifteen, having first gathered warm down jackets from the floor above, knowing not what they were or why we needed them.

But we soon did. Papa and Elise plunged us into winter. As we entered we saw a sea of white. Snow! Everywhere; it was so beautiful, glistening in the sunshine. It rested on trees, bushes and grass, on a nearby bench and way into the distance. Elise gave us thick leather gloves and we'd found 'wellies' in another cupboard.

Papa was laughing with Elise. "If Mac's going to make us work through rest days we might as well enjoy it."

They walked hand in hand along what seemed to be a path that had a low wooden fence outlining it. I was deep in thought, when something cold and wet hit me and disintegrated on my jacket, splashing my face. John was grinning mischievously and burst out laughing as I picked up a handful of snow and aimed it at him. I ducked another which came from nowhere and

132

then sent one in Papa's direction. Our snowball fight lasted for ages, then Elise started to roll a larger ball through the new snow.

"I'm making a snowman!" she called from the other side. "I haven't done this since I was a child. Paris doesn't get snow very often. Come and help. We need another smaller ball."

"Ah, you know about Paris, then? We weren't supposed to say anything to prejudice your choice of future home," Papa called.

"It came out that first morning, when Elise was showing me all the new clothes and was a secret bond between us. Where do you think I got Papa from? Surely it's not that important, not now anyway. To hell with Mac and his rules."

"Come on Carli!" John was rolling a second ball, which was plonked on top of the first. Elise showed us how to add extra snow to make the correct shape. When it was done she went over to the computer terminal and politely asked for a hat, scarf, pipe, a carrot and two small pieces of coal. All these were taken over to our snowman. His mouth had been made using some small stones we found under the snow on the path. We used the coal for eyes and his nose was the carrot. With the pipe, hat and scarf, he was perfect.

"Our first snowman, we should give him a name."

John moved the outside stones of his mouth so that they turned down, "We'll call him Grouchy, because he looks like Mac, except for the pipe."

"You're shivering. Let's go somewhere warmer." Papa nodded at Elise and she led us by the hand outside into the corridor, where we abandoned our coats and weatherproof footwear.

"Arles," she said, when we re-entered, "in the summer. In the distance you can see the river and the bridge."

We were surrounded by sunflowers. "I had no idea they were so huge." I was dwarfed by their size. I'd seen them in paintings and knew what they were but in reality they were amazing. No wonder Van Gough loved them.

We walked through this field and stood at the edge of a meadow full of wild flowers blooming in the long grass. Then, as we approached a narrow tributary you could see there was a large quantity of watercress with its tiny white flowers impeding the flow. The trees were beautiful and in full leaf. Pink snakes-head fritillaries, grew in large clusters in this shaded area, their bell like heads dancing in the breeze.

The sun was bright and it felt warm and comforting on my face and arms. Was this what Brisbane was like? Back in the meadow we sat on the grass. Elise told us about Arles and it's association with the old French artists. "They came here because of the light," she said. "The air is very clear and creates a perfect light for painting." I could tell she knew about the subject.

"Do you paint," I asked her out of the blue.

"Not very well, but I enjoy using water colours when I have the time. I paint with the twins. They splash a mass of colour everywhere with huge enthusiasm, then use their hands and get into an awful mess." She laughed with a far away expression; I guess she was missing Fabian and Xavier. I suppose I would, too, if they were mine. I found myself wanting to meet them, and wondered what they'd think of me.

Papa was saying that we needed to go and find a storm, whatever that was.

We collected waterproof jackets this time and umbrellas. This program was different to the others as it changed while we were there. It started with light summer rain, which gradually got heavier, turning to frozen globules called hail. Then Papa told us to close our umbrellas and hold on to them. We pulled our hoods up and the wind became stronger. The sky darkened as the rain got worse. Suddenly there was a bright flash of lightning. The whole sky lit up, followed by a terrifyingly loud crash of thunder. John was delighted but I wasn't so sure. It frightened the wits out of me. You could hear the thunder rolling around the sky. We were soaked. After a bit the rain eased; the sun had come out and there in the sky were the gorgeous colours of a rainbow, forming a huge arc across the sky. It flashed through my mind how glad I was that I could enjoy colour for what it was. Had I really missed the music it created? I hadn't thought about it for ages.

Then almost in an instant the rain stopped, the sun magically drying both us and the area around us. What an amazing phenomenon.

Time had gone so quickly and I had to admit that Mac had been right, this weather experience wasn't like any lesson I'd ever known. We'd all had a splendid morning. I had a sudden thought, "Will Grouchy still be there if we go back?"

Papa laughed. "No," he said. "Every visit to that program will start at the beginning with it's pure, white layer of snow. But you can build him again!"

Elise added, "The Holodecks are always fun to visit. There are so many programs, and you can, of course create your own. I needed to create the kitchen for your cookery lessons."

After lunch we spent a dull afternoon with Otto. I guess it wasn't his fault, but meteorology is not the most exciting of subjects. John enjoyed it, and, I think, spending time with his father, too. He's got more of a scientific brain than I have. He yelled at me to wake up a couple of times as my mind wandered. Not literally, but just sent a loud thought telepathically, if you get my meaning.

That evening we communicated only through telepathy, until Otto remarked that we were very quiet and he hoped we hadn't had a row! We'll need to think about not cutting people out in future, but it is so nice to be able to converse in a way that not even Mac can understand.

19

The violence of Earth

Sunday, 10th June 2265

It's over a week since I last wrote in my diary. I've decided it would be extremely boring if I continue writing every day as it happens. We are learning so much and yet most of it is experience, rather than fact. Papa says it's all part of our adjustment to life on Earth. So I will relate only the significant info, rather than the lot.

We spent most of last Sunday on our own and had a lovely day. We found fifteen two vacant and spent a couple of hours wandering through the fields in Arles, then sat in the sunshine reading. The Italian food in Romano's was delicious, especially their yummy ice cream. We pigged out and then went back later for some more.

All week we were being 'acclimatised', and it wasn't very nice. The worst thing was the first time we saw the news. I had no idea how horrible people could be to each other. The narrator went on about drug related crime and…. oh, it was ghastly. We've also seen a lot of films. A whole week of nastiness. I really don't want to think about it at all. We also learned about the first and second World Wars, all together not a very nice week at all. I was feeling pretty glum about everything.

Today was better. We spent the day with Pap and Elise, ending up in 629, their quarters, for a very yummy dinner. Otto was there as well, though what happened to Mac I don't know and don't care.

It is now a calender month since we left home. An interesting thought, it seems a lot longer. So much has happened, none of which I expected. Here I am on a starship with my father and stepmother, travelling to make a new life on Earth. I have no real idea what I am going into, only so pleased that John will be with me. I have absolute faith in him.

20

We make a decision

Sunday, June 17th 2265

We are now beginning our final few days on the Endeavour. Looking back over the last week, I'm not sure whether this is an attractive proposition or not. The whole time we have been discovering how horrible life really is on the mother planet. We finally learned about the terrible Third World War which wiped out large chunks of two continents. Whole cities completely destroyed. It's hard to believe, but the records and films are there. Millions died.

We learned about the creation of the World Council, which had lead to the appointment of the Guardians of Peace. This in turn brought forth their creation of their Utopian society on Mars. With our new-found knowledge of politics, was this Utopia pure communism?   No religion, no hierarchy. But is life there any better? Different? Yes. Peaceful? Yes. Sanitised? Yes. Almost prison-like? Perhaps, but is that worse than what we are going into? I look towards our journey's end on Thursday with trepidation. But can it be *so* bad, after all Papa and Elise live there and they are sane enough? My poor brain has been overloaded with misery recently, I don't know what to think or believe.

It's late to be awake and I should have written this tomorrow but can't sleep, so here I am, chatting away at nearly midnight.

Mac reappeared today. After another week of not seeing him he arrived, still in uniform, after lunch. He dismissed Papa, Elise and Otto and started to talk to us about our future plans.

I was immediately alienated. Why are the others not involved? He spoke about us continuing our education, although perhaps having some time out before university.

"A lot of young people go travelling and experience life before going back into study after completing school." (At least he'd stopped referring to us as children!)

Yes, I thought, but none of them have travelled to or experienced life on Mars. I picked up something similar from Andrew – it's no good, I still think of him as Andrew, he'll never be John to me. I wonder if he feels the same about Carli. Suddenly I realised neither of us were listening to Mac; it was like an off switch. Something isn't right about all this. If it was a joint conspiracy, why were the others excluded? Telepathically I told him to drop these thoughts and listen to Mac, who was going on about The Far East and South America. Whatever happened he must not find out about our telepathic communication; we had to be careful around him.

"Have you thought about which university? Where you want to live?" A change of subject, perhaps to catch us out as we'd obviously not been paying attention.

"The Sorbonne!" I came back with instantly. "Is it in France or Switzerland? Somewhere European, I'm sure." One of us had needed to say something and it was, as usual, the first thing that came into my head – perhaps not so daft after all.

I thanked my lucky stars that I'd been looking up university information last night on my e-Tec. It was only an idea and I needed to see what Andrew wanted before plunging into anything – but we didn't have to decide here and now, did we?

Mac enthused about Oxford and Cambridge; went on and on. How wonderfully British they were with their ancient heritage and traditions, punting on the river….. blah, blah. Oh shut up Mac and leave us alone!

We escaped about half an hour later, having had a dull lecture on his own travels in Argentina, Brazil and Japan and his time at Cambridge with our fathers. He had told us nothing we wanted to know, about what our real purpose on Earth would be and, for that matter, why he and James and Otto couldn't just get on and do it themselves anyway.

It was still early. In Romano's we found a private corner table and unwound over ice cream sundaes.

"What's going on, Jay?" (So I had been right; maybe we could be ourselves, Andrew and Jay when we were together?) "All that rubbish about travel and British culture? It's in Paris, by the way. Thought you knew that."

"Yes, I did, but I didn't want to let on and perhaps let slip that Papa and Elise would be there for company. He seems to be very dismissive of them sometimes, almost treats them as inferior. Have you noticed? Perhaps it's the old rivalry between the arts and science?"

We sat in silence for a moment and I suddenly

remembered something that Elise said on that first morning, 'Don't let them bully you.' And I thought, no, I'm not going to let Mac persuade me to do anything I don't want to do.

"Have you thought about where we should live?" Andrew asked.

"Anywhere, just so long as that awful man isn't there!" I almost shouted with venom.

"I wondered if we could… er... stay with someone for a while," he was being cagey and almost dropping a hint; not in the least bit Andrew-like! Then I picked up his line of thought.

"We could ask them, but is that what you really want?"

"Put it this way. If we're on our own we'll be out of our depth. Get utterly depressed and jump off the nearest skyscraper!"

That's my Andrew, I thought, no mincing words. "I admit I had thought about it, but they're my family and it might become a bit overpowering for you."

"What, James, Elise and a couple of four year old brats? Na! I can handle them. Besides I like J and E and have a lot of respect for them. And she's a fabulous cook!"

Again I thought, please, Andrew, never lose your sense of humour.

With teenage impulsiveness, we'd dashed back to the lounge. They weren't there. Otto was, though, talking to Mac whose back was to us. Otto saw us but didn't acknowledge, so we rapidly retreated to 629. Again no luck.

"Arles!" We chorused.

Third time lucky. The programme was running, so

we burst in, not knowing the correct protocol for the interruption of a set. We found them sitting with a glass of wine in the middle of our meadow.

"Hello, we were just talking about you," Elise smiled. She seemed pleased to see us; so did Papa. Andrew and I did a telepathic you ask, no you he's your Dad, thing, took a deep breath and then, speaking alternately as a double act we asked.

"Do you think….?" Andrew started.

"Would it be possible?" -me.

"Can we….." Andrew again.

"Please may we go to Paris with you on Thursday?" I looked at Papa and then Elise. They were laughing. Elise held out her arms to me.

"We wanted to ask you to come and stay," she said, "but didn't want to put you under any pressure. Life has been so intense for you since we met. You will be very welcome to stay as long as you like. Mama and Papa will be delighted to meet you and so will the boys."

We talked about Paris for ages, sitting on the grass. I would like to visit Arles. Would it really be like this? The sun was setting and it was becoming cooler also time was running out and soon the next visitors would be arriving to run another programme. I would have some happy memories of the holodeck with Papa and Elise.

"I will make supper, if you'd like to come back to 629?"

"No," Andrew surprised me, "we'll cook for you!"

I am starting to fall asleep and have already made a few mistakes, so I will end here and write again soon. We'll see what this week has to offer.

21

I ask Mac the big one

Wednesday, June 20th 2265

I'm not really sure why I am writing this. Nothing new has gone on recently only more of the same acclimatisation, but I want to think about things laterally and it's easier if I write them down. I may well decide to scrap this when I read it through later.

This is our last day on the Endeavour. Tomorrow we dock at the space station, from there to be transferred to Florida in the United States of America. Mac was not at all pleased that we would be leaving with James and Elise. I think he wanted to keep us here on the ship for longer, but we were adamant, and so we leave in the afternoon, with the others. I have no doubt he will be issuing them with instructions to keep us in order.

I've been trying to work out exactly what Mac is asking us to do. As I see it he wants us to expose the V machine and how the Guardians are using it on Mars. What I can't understand is why he and James and Otto don't go ahead and do it themselves? I understand that Otto is bound by Official Secrets laws and that no-one is supposed to know about it, but in that case how do we explain how we found out? And who is going to believe us anyway? If it came out that Otto had informed not only us but Mac and James too, then he would be charged with treason, wouldn't he? Banished forever to Titan and hard labour. I think this whole exposure idea is Mac's. He seems to be the one in charge the way he bosses the others about. And then there was his dismissal of the others on Sunday. What was that all about?

What about the use of cloning to make perfect specimens? That's definitely his speciality and he's been involved in trials for 'ageing' the new clones. How would the population of, say Paris, feel about cloning, well, killing any one who wasn't perfect. I might as well be clinical about it, it makes it easier to reason if I can think in a detached way. I know how I feel about it, but what about ordinary human beings who have grown up in the violence of Europe, America or anywhere else for that matter? We've seen all these films and news reports but still haven't met anyone from Earth, except Cmdr Johnson. We have no idea what life is really like. What the general public think or say; how they might react?

We were talking about this yesterday. We have gone back to being Andrew and Jay, by the way, regardless of what Mac says, but only to ourselves, when we're on our own and here, in my diary. Elsewhere we must be careful not to slip up. There's always telepathy, so we very seldom have to use our new names, even in company.

There is another side to all this, one which we are only now beginning to learn about, and that is Religion. We've been reading various books on the subject and have discovered that there are many different forms of religion throughout the world. Most use the idea of a higher being and talk about faith and destiny, but surely these gods, to use a generic term, are all beings of love and would therefore not approve of killing people, sick, injured, old or…. anyone. I wonder what the response would be from the hierarchy of these organisations. I must ask Papa and Elise at our next session. Perhaps the way to report what happens on Mars is to approach the religious organizations first?

I think it has been quite a difficult subject for Elise and Papa to teach. Elise was brought up within the Catholic Church under the umbrella of the Christian Religion. I am not sure how strong her beliefs are but I know it's a subject which is dear to her heart; I can feel it. Andrew would say I'm talking rubbish, but I'm sure I'm right. But I don't know how Papa feels about the subject, he is quite different in his approach. He is matter of fact and informative in a very detached way.

He goes into the history of religious wars and conflicts over the hundreds, no thousands of years and their influence on our way of life. I'm not sure what I want to believe, if anything, but I am keen to find out more.

We have been on this ship for four weeks. We've been tutored nearly every day and there's still so much that we don't know. But I do feel different in myself, as though I've grown up a lot and suddenly become an adult. My writing, too, has changed. I know this entry is different because it's not 'a day in the life of' but a philosophical one, while I try to sort out my ideas, but that isn't quite what I mean. If I look back to the beginning and compare, I think I am writing less as a child now. Also the relationship between Andrew and me has changed. Is it the telepathy that makes me feel that we are almost one person? Maybe two parts of a whole might be a better way to put it? It is difficult not to take what the other is thinking for granted and I sometimes have to stop myself from assuming too much.

I have begun writing again. Yes, I can hear you thinking, what's this if it's not writing? No, I mean stories. Stories about living on Mars. No, it's not another diary, just memories of things we did. Some of them are from school; trips out and things. I think it's important not to forget where we've come from and what life was like. I wrote about the 'Sameness of Mars.' Maybe it will help later with 'The Great Exposure'. Yesterday I recalled a day Mum and I spent together. I do miss her loads, and get all emotional if I dwell on it. This time we were going round the art gallery. I wish I could see those same paintings again in colour. I did take off my glasses for a quick peep a few times, but it's not the same. That's how I remembered the yellow of the sunflowers. I wonder if Turner painted his sunsets from reality? I can't wait to find out.

I'm supposed to be trying to work out what we are going to do, but I'm getting nowhere fast; only throwing up more questions. I might eventually decide to delete this section, but I guess it's a useful bit of background info.

We have a later start today, which is why I've been able to write this before getting up. Now I must get dressed and meet Andrew for breakfast, we've promised ourselves pancakes and maple syrup.

It was while Andrew was fetching our breakfast that Mac arrived and I found myself alone at the table with him. I looked round and there was a queue at the replicators, so I made a decision to go for it and asked,

"Why can't you, Papa and Otto not confront the Guardians yourselves and then tell the world what they are doing?" This was the big one, the question we'd be thinking about for more than four weeks. Why neither of us had come out with it before I couldn't say. Nerves? Perhaps. Or subconsciously not wanting to know the answer.

"You do pick your moments, Carli. Have you been taking lessons from John?"

I'd obviously surprised him, but it was he who told me to be assertive.

"The answer is simple. Otto and I are both known to the Guardians. We would be imprisoned and exiled before we could broadcast anything. As to James, he is far too weak to undertake such a task! He is only involved because of you! Ah, there are Otto and the others, and John is returning with your breakfast. I will see you before you disembark. Goodbye."

"Too weak? What do you mean by that?" I yelled after him but he'd gone.

I sat there, astonished and furious. Now I understood their dismissal yesterday. I wonder if Papa knew what Mac really thought of him? I must put it out of my mind or Andrew will pick it up and I need to tell him about it later, not now with everyone here. You have no idea how difficult it is not to think about something when you really want to. I looked up and forced myself to greet everyone as normally as I could.

"Here we are, pancakes and maple syrup, yummy!" Andrew looked quizzically at me and asked what was up. Later, please. Not now, I transmitted, as the others sat down. Thank goodness he didn't pursue the matter.

Breakfast took an age. I don't think Papa and Elise noticed anything wrong and Otto was too enthusiastically eating sausages and scrambled eggs to observe anything. I like pancakes, I thought. I concentrated hard on remembering how to make them. This kept my brain occupied, but I missed some of the conversation.

Andrew interrupted me, "How about it? We probably won't get another chance." Exasperated, he signed. "You've missed it, haven't you? We've been invited to the bridge!"

"Oh, wow! That would be fantastic." But it was said without genuine enthusiasm. "When?"

Otto answered. "In about an hour's time," he said, looking at his watch. "I'll meet you here at 10.50.

"We'll see you later, James and I are going to pack. This afternoon I'll help you with yours."

Packing? It would wait. I grabbed Andrew's hand and headed for the door.

"Hey, slow down! What's the hurry?"

"Mac!" I yelled, "can't you guess?" and ran towards the lift, which closed in front of me so I careered down the stairs, Andrew in close pursuit. By the time I got to 513 I was out of breath and had a stitch, but was much calmer.

"OK, so tell me what happened."

"I asked him. The one thing we'd wanted to know. 'Why couldn't he, Otto and James have gone to the council with their findings and exposed the Guardians themselves? Why did they need us to do it? Do you know what that despicable man said? What that disgusting pig of a man came up with, word for word: 'The answer is simple. Otto and I are both known to the

Guardians. We would be imprisoned and exiled before we could broadcast anything. As to James, he is far too weak to undertake such a task! He is only involved because of you!' He said Papa is weak? I know he may not be the perfect gentleman and has had a bit of a dodgy past but he's the only civilised one of them. How dare he be so insulting? How dare he be so critical, so disloyal, so two faced, so, so............ Ooh! I can't think of anything bad enough for him!"

"I can but you'd only moan at me." Andrew sat opposite me, staring. I glared at him and shouted, "Not this time I wouldn't!"

Oddly enough he didn't. All he transmitted to me was, 'Jay, you're lovely when you're angry. With you're red hair you're so full of fire.' The rat!

I shut out his remark, pretended not to understand, so when he suggested, Romano's, I replied, "Why not?" Then suddenly realised the time.

"No, we must go back to Effie, it's nearly a quarter to eleven."

"Jay, do you want to do this? I mean, I could always say you had a headache or something."

"No, I've got over the initial shock now. Thanks for listening. We'll talk about it, but later. Also I have to think what I'm going to say to Papa, and when."

The visit to the Bridge was amazing. I've only ever seen holographic projections of one before and that was an old Star ship, nothing like this state of the arts inter-galaxy vessel. Captain Andersen was kind and not at all condescending, Otto was on good terms with him, they had known each other for a long time. I am beginning to think that I'd like to get to know Otto better. He has an amazing mind, knows an incredible amount about a lot of things. It's a shame our time with him has almost run out.

Sorry, back to the bridge. It was a lot bigger than I was expecting. We were introduced to several bridge officers, Helm, Communications Officer, Science Officer and someone called The First Officer, who is next in command after the Captain. We were there for almost an hour, even got to sit in the captain's chair. The communications system was explained to us and we had the most fabulous view of the Universe. This enormous screen has a two-way use so that other ships have visual contact, too. In a discussion this can be important, it's sometimes vital to be able to read your opponent's body language. (Not my words but the captain's which I don't fully understand.) We looked forward, towards the ever growing planet of Earth; so beautiful.

Andrew was in his element. Maybe he should become an officer on a Galaxy starship one day. But then we have to expose what the Guardians are planning and I guess after that no-one will want to know either of us.

I haven't thought about this consequence before. We could end up as exiles. Does that really matter? Elise and Papa would never forsake us and I'm sure there will be others who think the same way as us, even if they don't know about it yet. No, think positive, everything will work out fine.

In my usual dreamy way I missed some of the more detailed information, but I'm sure Andrew would have told me if this was noticeable.

Afterwards Otto took us to the science labs and showed us his project work from earlier on. 'Fraid that went way above my head. But he was nice about it and wasn't patronising. Maybe he is more like Andrew than I gave him credit for. Someone asked if he would be able to stay for an hour or so to check on something, so we left him to it and made our way back towards Romano's, thinking about a nice Italian lunch. You know for someone who's never eaten food until four weeks ago, Andrew is becoming very exacting about it. He is also a better cook than me, as last night's meal proved. Maybe he can do most of it later, when we're on our own.

We both wanted to say goodbye to Arles. We'd checked the bookings for fifteen two and found a spare two hours and quickly bagged them. So, after a hurried lunch and equipped with a bottle of fruit juice, some of Andrew's favourite chocolate, my e-Tec and his reader, we relaxed in our meadow.

And that's where I am now, enjoying the sunshine, writing and thinking how sad the people on Mars are to never see this. Never needing to put on a coat or wellies for snow or rain, or seeing a rainbow. Never to have the exciting choice of what to wear for a special occasion, think about changing their hair style to go with a different outfit; or even owning a different outfit for that matter.

"Hello! Mind if we interrupt? We couldn't resist when we saw the program was our one set in Arles, we were sure it would be you."

"Not much time left, Papa. We have to leave soon. The next person is due in….. oh ……. thirty minutes. I was catching up on my diary and this morning's Bridge visit. Andrew's found some ancient book or other from the twentieth century. It's such a nice place to sit and unwind. I didn't realise you'd written the program. But, of course I should have guessed. Is Arles a special place for you two?"

Andrew was trying to contact me and stop my mindless rambling, but then I asked, "Why is Mac so disparaging of you?" Oops, I'm getting more like Andrew every day.

Papa looked thoughtful, "What's he been saying? He has a tendency to be arrogant at times."

I looked to Andrew who characteristically raised his eyebrow. I may as well carry on.

"Earlier this morning I asked him why you, he and Otto couldn't inform on the activities of the Guardians? Why it must be us? His exact words were:- 'The answer is simple. Otto and I are both known to the Guardians. We would be imprisoned and exiled before we could broadcast anything. As to James, he is far too weak to undertake such a task! He is only involved because of you!'"

Papa was thoughtful, "That's interesting, I've often wondered why he kept me in the loop. So simple as that, eh? It never occurred to me. It's probably true, but not quite in the way it seems. You see, I do not have a technical mind and therefore the ability to comprehend everything that I would need to know as an informer."

Now, *that* I did understand. "But he inferred that you were a coward! It was so insulting!"

"No, not really, he is just a pompous ass. Full of puffed-up superiority and self importance, not an uncommon occurrence with scientists and their attitude to others."

I flashed a murderous look at Andrew – don't even think about it, I transmitted!

Papa looked at me, concerned. "Don't let it upset you, Carli."

Elise had been deep in thought. "You said 'his exact words.' Did you mean that?"

"Yes," I replied, almost irritably, "I have a complete memory or total recall or whatever you call it. But that's not the point. Why should he treat you as inferior?"

I picked up that Andrew was telling me to let it go. He also seemed to think that Elise was quite impressed. I saw her expression and decided to back down. If Papa really wasn't bothered then why should I be?

The three minute buzzer sounded for the end of our program. We'd previously decided to return to Romano's for Ice Cream Sundae's as we'd missed the sweet course at lunch time. Now we weren't sure. Elise resolved the problem by suggesting Romano's for us all, decision made.

She was intrigued by my 'revelation' as she put it. To me it was nothing special, I'd always been able to remember things clearly. Maybe that's why I enjoyed writing so much and hated card games as they were no mystery to me. But she was adamant that this was something very special, and Papa described it as 'an incredibly useful asset'.

I've just yawned and have had to re-write the last paragraph. It's late and I must get some sleep. There's nothing much to report about the evening, our last, which we spent with Elise, Papa and Otto and, thankfully, no Mac.

22

Last day on Endeavour

Thursday 21st June 2265

Elise arrived early; she was carrying two very large holdalls. Apparently Otto had organised Andrew into doing his packing as well. Although we'd been here for a month I didn't have that much to pack. I'd bought very little, except a fabulous green top which I fell in love with and Andrew said made my eyes light up. Oh, and a short denim dress that I refused to wear without jeans underneath and another red one, which I'm still not sure about. Sorry, getting sidetracked again.

I emptied all the drawers and she folded and put everything into the bags. It didn't take long. There was a smaller bag for toiletries and another prettier one into which I put my necklaces and hair slides. And there was my world, in two bags sitting on the bed. It felt so final. Different from any other departure. I was missing Mum.

Before I could dwell on it Andrew arrived. "What! Not even dressed! At least you've packed, so we'll be able to do what we want this morning."

A short time later we were deciding what to have for breakfast. "Coffee in a bowl and hot croissants." I had developed the French habit of dunking my croissants. Elise did this too.

"Tomorrow I shall make real coffee and Mama will buy fresh croissants from the Boulangerie," she said.

"Ah. Very French," observed Otto, munching his bacon butty.

"Where will you be, tomorrow?" Andrew asked his father.

"Geneva. Preparing myself for an interview with The Guardians. Can't say I'm looking forward to it."

"Do you know what it's about?"

"Not sure. Could be a number of things."

"I hope you can manage a stop over in Paris before you return States-side. The twins would like to see their Uncle Otto again. They still have the spaceship you made them all those months ago. They won't let anyone dismantle it and put the bricks back in the box." Elise continued, "Do come, if you can fit us in."

I started to think about him as a family man and to wonder what Andrew's childhood was like.

"There should be time. I will let you know. John, I have something to give you at lunch time, until then I have things to do and will see you all later."

We watched him leave. I couldn't imagine him as 'Uncle' Otto, playing with four year old twins. But if they'd kept his spaceship, he must have made a favourable impression on them. Or maybe it was a really good model, he was, after all an engineer!

We made our way to the observation lounge, which was surprisingly empty. I'd have thought that everyone would have wanted to see Earth as we approached the space station. It filled the screen and was so beautiful. Again I thought of my colour music and imagined what it would have been like. I thought

156

back to the Temeraire and Catalina, wondering how she was doing, learning how to play with both hands and whether she was playing, what was now, her colour music.

Andrew sat beside me. He was deep in thought and I picked up a complete muddle of info from him.

"Wonder what he wants? I'll miss him. Got used to him being around. Know him better. Will we ever see him again?" he asked me.

"I hope so," I said and I meant it. I was pleased that my initial hatred of Otto had disintegrated, becoming a warm tolerance and admiration.

It was not long after that the man himself walked in and came over to us.

"Mind if I sit down? Andrew, no, John, I have written my contact details for you. Keep it safe but it would be wise to memorise, if you can."

"Don't insult me!" He gave his father that familiar raised left eyebrow look. "Is it shorter than the periodic table?"

"You make your point. Never underestimate a mathematician Carli."

"Can I ask you something?" I was wondering why he needed to pass his details on to Andrew, when we were supposed not to have any more contact with anyone on Mars. Also why he hadn't done this at breakfast or lunch, but chosen a time when he knew we would be alone. Not only that but he'd taken the trouble to find us. His reply was interesting, although he took a few moments to answer.

"I have sensed, not from you, John, more from Carli, that you do not like Mac. I also have an underlying uneasiness. There may come a time when you need to get hold of me, without going through Mac. Simple as that."

"Dad, can we talk about this mission of ours, this great exposure. We still know so little about it. Mac said you've been planning this for sixteen years. It doesn't make sense, we would only have been two at the time."

"In my work with the Guardians and the development of the Vaporiser, it very early on became apparent what they would use it for. It was then, in conversation with Mac and James that we realised we had to devise a way of stopping them. Already it has been in use far too long, since 2250."

"We know, we found the re-classification detail when we were on the Temeraire." I interrupted.

"The decision was made to make clones of you both. Jay because of her colour/music oddity, which eventually the Guardians would have picked up on as an abnormality and want to destroy. Andrew was cloned for practical reasons. When the time came for Jay to be on the Temeraire you would have each other. Mac went to great lengths to arrange that, as you know."

"Poor, Mum," put in Andrew. "Sorry," he added as his father frowned at the interruption. "Why us?"

"Carli, you are unique. You were the only person who could ever have discovered that the Temeraire never left the orbit of Mars. This was something that your father realised and explained to us, but thankfully the Guardians would not have known. But you needed Andrew to goad you into exploring and discovering what was happening. Mac guided you very carefully through everything you found out. You were monitored to be sure you hadn't missed anything. I'm extremely proud of you both. You were an excellent team, still are."

"But, Dad, how are we going to expose these Guardians?" Andrew was being slow to catch on again, but I kept quiet.

"You are the only survivors of the Temeraire. There will never be others, or another chance to do this. You have to tell your version of the events. To the press, the media and anyone who will listen…...."

"Hello, Papa!" I shouted and waved as James and Elise entered the lounge. I gave Otto apologetic look Otto to say sorry for the sharp interruption. He understood.

"Where shall we go for our last lunch?" Elise was looking very smart in her red top and black trousers again.

Mac arrived, too and informed us that he would be in Paris next week on the 27th, Wednesday, and would need to meet with us. All very formal, I thought, unenthusiastically. Whatever.

Later Andrew and I sat together in companionable silence, waiting for the ship to dock.

"This is a big step, Jay. We have no idea what we're really going into. We are suppose to be enlightening the world about the behaviour of their esteemed governmental guardians. We have no idea how we're going to do it. We don't even have any proof!"

I smiled at him, "Yes we do," I thought. "We have my diary."

23

Paris

Saturday, June 23rd 2265

Things have been so busy and exciting since we left the Endeavour that I haven't yet had time to catch up.

The shuttle that took us to Florida didn't take long, but we would have had to wait two days for the next flight to Paris. Papa decided that it would be a good idea to go to New York as we would get an earlier direct flight from there. But we did have time for a quick visit to the space museum. How vast were those original rockets? I guess they needed all that fuel until the anti-gravity method of propulsion was developed. The early moon landing craft looked so *old*, almost like a giant insect with long legs. Probably very futuristic when it was built. They have rock from the moon and photographs taken on Mars, but nothing of Newton Aldrin and our lifestyle there. I wonder what people think about Martian life. Do they even know that there is a colony there?

Sight-seeing in New York was so amazing. I could write a whole book on this city. A jungle of skyscrapers; I especially liked the Chrysler building, it's so old, so elegant. I was disappointed with the planetarium. Having seen the real thing it was a bit tame, but Andrew and I have decided we must come back to 'The Big Apple' again. I'll write about it in detail then and carry on with my diary now.

The flight from there was 'super-sonic' across the Atlantic, and was over so quickly, arriving early this morning. Early enough to be at Papa and Elise's for breakfast. Also early enough to completely confuse me about time zones as we arrived before we'd left? Duh? My brain is totally upskittled, I'll get Andrew to explain it all to me sometime.

At the house they were expecting us. We met Elise's parents, Henri and Françoise and, of course, the twins Xavier and Fabian, my new family. Yet again I felt myself being overwhelmed and tears started to form with that prickly feeling at the top of my nose, but I blinked them away and gripped Andrew's hand.

There was no time for awkwardness as we were ushered into the enormous kitchen for 'le petit déjeuner' as breakfast will always be called while we are here. Even though everyone speaks English certain words are sacrosanct according to Papa. I think it's a lovely tradition.

I discovered another French expression still used when Françoise asked me if John was my petit ami?

"You know, dear, your young man." She explained when I looked quizzically at her.

I explained that we were only good friends, we'd travelled together on the Endeavour and added that his father was Otto, who they probably had met. She gave me a very 'knowing' sort of look which I have yet to interpret.

Sitting there, looking round I suddenly realised the familiarity of it all. "It's the kitchen we used on the

Endeavour!" I exclaimed.

"Well, I had to create one for you and this seemed the most sensible one to use as a model. James and I designed it when we had the house refurbished two years ago. If you are looking for anything you'll find it in the same place as the one you remember. Although here I have more serving dishes and general equipment. And now, if you are all finished perhaps Fabian, Xavier, you will show Carli and John the rest of the house.

They were delighted to oblige but only got as far as their playroom to show us a large model of a galaxy type spaceship made out of plastic bricks all stuck together. It was spectacular, no wonder they wouldn't dismantle it.

"Uncle Otto made it. Is he your Papa?" they demanded of Andrew.

"He is indeed and we are hoping he will be here next week."

"Goody! And you are our big sister, Carli? Why haven't we met you before? Your Papa is our Papa, but who is your Mama and where is she?"

As soon as Andrew was questioned I'd been expecting this and was ready with an answer which I hoped would satisfy them and also maybe Elise's parents, as I didn't know how much we'd be able to tell them. No time to consult with Papa, I needed an answer.

"I lived a long way away with my Mama, in Australia, but now I have come to Europe to be with you and Papa, and to go the University where Papa teaches."

All this was said with my fingers crossed behind my back. I'm useless at lying but I don't think they

162

spotted anything wrong. I must remember to tell Papa and Elise soon, though. Andrew signed, "Well done. Good thinking."

A bit later, while Elise and I were unpacking, I explained what I had done. I hoped she wouldn't be annoyed because I'd lied to the boys.

"Mama and Papa know the full truth. We thought it was only fair to tell them and you can trust them absolutely to keep your secret. But you did the right thing with the boys. To satisfy their curiosity was the best thing to do. That will be the cover story that will get out. Though you may need to swat up a little on life in the Australian outback. I'm only sorry that we didn't think about this subject before."

Theirs is a lovely house. From the outside it looks quite old, but inside it has been made very modern. I've never seen such beautiful furniture or fabrics before, and in such gorgeous colours. I'm glad I can appreciate these easily now. They also have a very pretty garden. The twins proudly showed me their precious sunflower plants. They are impatiently waiting for them to grow.

I could go on and on about this delightful day, but it would become very boring and probably repetitive, so I will leave it to your imagination and say goodnight.

24

Otto has devastating news

Tuesday, June 26th 2265

We've been sightseeing. Yesterday Henri and Françoise wanted to show us their city, and took us proudly around. They have lots of energy and were quite happy climbing up and down all the steps in Montmartre, though we also went on the funicular. I can't believe how old some of the buildings are. We sat by the Seine and had a picnic lunch. This was Andrew's idea as we'd passed a shop selling small pizza's and yummy pastries. We found fresh strawberries at an outside stall.

We both like Henri and Françoise. They have been so kind to us, and, indeed it is they who will continue our education, both being retired lecturers. A perfect union of the generations.

I had worried about how we'd fit in living with James and Elise. Would we be in the way? Would they get fed up with us? But I needn't have. We're all one big happy family. Heck! That sounds *so* cheesy! (One of Papa's expressions that caused much amusement at first.)

Mac rang to say he had been delayed and would have to stay in the US, but left us a message that he would be in Paris third week in August and would see us then. Ghastly thought!

Otto, however, did arrive this morning. He was carrying a huge box, which he immediately gave to the boys, telling them to unload it in their playroom. Two minutes later they were back beseeching Uncle Otto to come and build them another space ship.

"Now, children, you must let him at least have a cup of coffee first," Elise was laughing and said to Otto. "If you bring them a big box of bricks, what do you expect?"

Henri, who had arrived earlier, suggested that they might like to play football in the park for an hour. They found their outdoor shoes and the football and waited for him by the door, urgently jumping up and down. Henri nodded to James, who grinned thankfully.

"How did you get on?" he asked Otto. Elise had disappeared upstairs and I signed to ask Andrew if he thought we should do the same.

Almost as if he understood, his father said, "No, stay. This concerns both of you as well." He looked preoccupied as he sat on a kitchen chair. "The Guardians want me to supervise the building of ten Vaporisers."

Andrew broke the silence. "Where? When? How long?"

"Eastern Europe. Three to six. Asap."

I wished they'd stop talking in shorthand! They were so alike. I looked at Andrew and gave him what I thought was my best French shrug.

"Surely even you can follow this!" was his mean retort. Then said, as if he was addressing a child, "They will be manufactured in Eastern Europe as soon as possible and will take between three and six months to complete. Depends on availability of parts?" Otto nodded.

I was about to go and sulk in the other room, when he touched my arm and said, "Sorry, Jay. Bit shocked. OK?" I nodded, grudgingly. I thought he'd grown out of that.

"I think we're all shocked. This is devastating news. I am right in thinking this will lead to trials on Earth?"

"Can only mean that, James. We now have to come up with a way to stop them."

"I was thinking about this earlier, Papa, before we left Endeavour. Would it be possible to approach the heads of the religious organisations?" They all looked at me.

Otto seemed sceptical but Papa thought it could work. "The difficulty is getting access to people like the Pope. They are all surrounded by officials and the amount of red tape involved would be prohibitive. It could take months just to establish contact..........."

I was trying not to ask what red tape had to do with it.

"It isn't as though we have any proof of what is happening on the Temeraire," he continued.

"There is my diary," I said in a small voice.

"Sorry, dear, what did you say?" James had said this and I could see he was interested.

"While we were on board I kept a diary. It's on my e-Tec, I'll get it."

When I returned they were arguing. Not aggressively, but stating opinions as to whether a teenage girl's diary would be of any use at all. Otto was dismissive, Papa wanted to see what was in it and

166

Andrew sat patiently on the kitchen table swinging his legs, waiting for me.

I put it down next to him, then opened it and found my entry for Tuesday 22nd May. Leaving out the bits about Andrew's antics I read from where Mac asked us to tell him what we knew. As I read the room went quiet, a captive audience. I went on for a bit and then skipped to the following day, including stuff about their clandestine plot and more on cloning.

"It's all here, even finding the V machine," I said. "Would it be of any use?"

Before I could stop him Andrew picked me up and whirled me round the room, to my horror and the others amusement.

"Oh, you clever, clever girl!" Excited, he put me down.

"I could edit out anything personal."

"But is it really proof that these things are happening on Mars? They would only deny it. Call it a teenage girl's fantasy." Otto was still unenthusiastic.

"What if there were two copies? An identical one on Mars," I asked.

Andrew had picked up on my thought trail. "You mean you copied it onto the new e-Tec?" He'd guessed the answer and before I could stop him.........

"Andrew! Put me DOWN!"

I recovered my dignity and stopped giggling. "I transferred it to a miniature Mem-Tic and hid it in the old case. It's not easy to find and may never be, but Mac didn't spot it when he put the new one in the old case, so it must still be there. Is there any way my clone could be helped to discover it?"

"The Temeraire 'docks' on the 27th July. I have to

be there to meet it. Perhaps I could help things along."

"How?" We chorused. Now it was Otto's turn to shrug.

"I'll just have to think of something. At least I shall be available on Mars if I'm needed. Very little can be done from here. The Endeavour is leaving for Jupiter Thursday, via Mars, and I'm booked on the Miami flight tomorrow. Now, if I'm not mistaken, our little chums are back and John and I have a space station to build."

The boys burst in, still jumping up and down. Were they always this excitable? "Uncle Otto, Uncle Otto, *please* come and build another space ship!"

Papa and I sat talking. "We need to think sideways and get some sort of plan together."

We all tried not to let Otto's news interfere with our day, but it was hard. My mind kept wandering and several times I had to bring myself back to reality.

The chaps decided to cook our main meal, Henri head chef with Andrew's help. James was with them preparing salad, but not Otto, I don't think he has ever cooked anything in his life. He was put in charge of the wine and produced two bottles Champagne from his luggage. We were to have our first taste of 'the real McCoy'!

It was a chance to discuss things with Otto. He asked me why I had hidden the diary from Mac. "Simple, don't trust him, never have. I'm sorry if that sounds judgemental, I know you've been friends for a long time and I don't mean to offend, but you did ask."

He wasn't bothered by my frankness. I'm not sure whether this surprised me or not. I had a feeling he agreed with me.

"I saw him in Geneva. He'd just got off the plane. I

was due to board my Paris flight, so he didn't see me. He did, of course know that I had a meeting with the Guardians. According to what he told James and me before leaving the Temeraire, the Guardians had no prior knowledge of his return to Earth, so how could he have been summoned unless he lied to us? Why would he do that?"

"He lied to us too. He cancelled his meeting with us tomorrow saying he was detained in the States."

"Jay, sorry, Carli, I think you're very wise not to trust him. I am inclined to be wary of him, too."

I'd already called John Andrew today so I explained that between us we were very much still Andrew and Jay. He understood and said how difficult it was to call his son by another name.

"You two are very good together. If anyone can sort out this mess then you can."

At least someone has faith in us, I'm not so sure myself.

25

My diary

Wednesday June 27th 2265

This morning Andrew, Papa and I started to form a plan. What we needed was publicity, preferably from a well respected source. The trouble with news on line is that you don't know how many people read it. The perfect solution was to be interviewed by the National Broadcasting Association or better still the International News Agency on prime time TV.

James knows people in television. He had been interviewed several times and would try his contact at the studio. Can it be that easy, I thought?

"You're forgetting that we only have your diary and, I think it would be better if we had both. We'll have to hope Dad can arrange for the other copy to be found." Andrew was deep in thought. "This is going to take time. Dad won't arrive on Mars until July twenty fourth or fifth. He's then got to be back here for the beginning of September for the building of the new machines. Could be only three months later the first of them will begin trials and then go into operation. If he brings the other diary back with him that puts a two month time scale on our plans. I don't think we should try to do much exposure before we have both diaries. It needs to be one big shock to everyone at the end of

August."

I could almost hear the cogs in his brain working this through.

James had listened to all this, quiet and thoughtful. "Jay, your diary, would you object to it being published? I'll need to read it first, but I have a good idea of the kind of book my publisher will accept. This might work well as there is a very controversial programme which launches new books and they get huge audiences."

"When's the programme?" Andrew and I said together. "What's it like?" I added.

"It schedules on the last Friday of each month, so that would be ….. August 31st. It is a live broadcast with studio audience. It covers all the arts and gets surprisingly high ratings. Their book of the month always causes a stir. If they will review it, we would be in with a chance.

"So, if you can get it published and launched at the end of August, Dad should be back in time for the big exposure!" Andrew was as excited as me.

"Papa, the other diary will end just before our transfer to the Endeavour. But it does cover the important bit, the discovery of everything. So this essential part of the diary is what should be published. I know exactly where I changed over to the new e-Tec."

Andrew was gazing at me like I was some new exhibition at the zoo.

26

Meanwhile …

Saturday July 14th 2265

I'm in love! It feels so wonderful and he is so amazing! It's a shame he doesn't know!

I've kept it a secret up till now, not even written it in my diary, but I can contain myself no longer. Does he fancy me? I'm not sure. I so hope so! He is so gorgeous, from his black curly hair to pink soled feet! I know he lives on the other side of the city, but I don't see that as a problem. Anyway, now that we've finished school we'll both be at the University together. That won't be until September, of course. Oh, I can't *wait* until then.

The only one I've told is Catalina. We have become besties, even though she's a bit younger than me. Since her piano has been in the lounge she has been very preoccupied with that, but it's OK as I can write or catch up on my reading. I'd rather be with Wes, but he is content to join the games with the others. I can sit and gaze at him though. I really like Catalina and trust her not to say anything to the others. We sit together and most of the time are totally inseparable. It's nice to find such a good friend, and completely by chance, having been thrown together on this return journey to Mars.

Delman and the twins have become pally but they

can be so sarcastic sometimes, all three of them. I think he's a bit dim, but that's good in a way as he misses a lot of our jokes, most of which, I'm ashamed to admit are against him. Well, he asks for it. He can be really nasty. Moraise and Saleena, or Mora and Sally, aren't so bad, just influenced by him.

I was thinking the other day about us. We are all known by nicknames now - even Delman is Del - except Andrew. He's a strange one. I think he's very clever. Whenever I've gone over to see what he is doing he's working out some sort of mathematical equation. He has a whole pile of maths books with him. Yuk! Can't stand maths, never was very good at it. No, English is my subject. I want to be a writer when I grow up. What an odd thing to say. I am grown up, at least I'm eighteen and can make my own decisions. But I don't feel it somehow, I still feel like a child inside, although I wouldn't admit it to anyone.

There is a new game here called Monopoly. Someone found it a few weeks ago. It was one of the others who showed them all how to play. I should explain about 'the others'. They are about our age, maybe a bit older. They were here before us and are very dull and boring. The two girls are both very plain and, well, ordinary, unmemorable. They never do anything with their mousey hair to change it, I don't think they even brush it, for that matter. And the three boys are equally nondescript. One has fairish hair and grey eyes and the others are dark haired and have brown eyes. I don't even know their names, probably because they aren't interesting enough to warrant them! Oh dear, that sounds awful, doesn't it? I shouldn't be so horrible. Mum would definitely not like that.

I wonder how she is? I've been thinking a lot about her lately, wanting to tell her about Wesley, ask her advice. I wonder if she was ever in love? Of course she was, she married Dad didn't she? I wonder why they really split up and where he is, if he's even still alive?

27

Back to Mars

Saturday July 21st 2265

It has been a horrible day! Horrible! Horrible! Horrible!

It began yesterday really. We were all in the lounge, after third pill time. Del and the twins were playing a game together. Cat and I were talking, when Wes came over. He sat down with us and then asked Catalina if she would like to watch the film with him later. I could not believe my ears when she said "Yes!"

If that's not betrayal, I don't know what is. I feel so wretched and haven't spoken to her since. She did try to talk to me this morning; said she was sorry but she'd liked him too. Even said that all was fair in love and war. Rubbish! She knew exactly how I felt about him. Well, as far as our friendship is concerned, END OF!!!

Sunday

I was sitting in the lounge alone this morning, feeling miserable, when a strange thing happened. Andrew came over. He brought up the three dimensional chess game that was integral with the table between us, and asked if I wanted to play. Why not, I thought. What's more I won, too. Although I have a feeling that he let me, as he easily took the next three games. I did give him a run for his money on the fourth, though. He wasn't very chatty, but I was quite glad of that. When the others left to watch Mora and Sally go through their gymnastics routines in the room next door, he smiled at me and asked, "What's wrong? You seem so sad today and you've been avoiding Catalina. Has she upset you?"

I didn't know what to say. I mean, I know girls have crushes on boys, but do boys have crushes on girls? Would he understand? Probably not and I didn't want to look pathetic, so I just said that we'd fallen out.

"Thought as much. Oh well, it'll all blow over, or not. If not, does it really matter as we shall only be together for another week, less than that now? Don't let her get to you, Jay."

He's right, isn't he? Why should I be miserable?

"You did let me win that first game, didn't you?"

"Of course. You needed cheering up. Besides, you're much prettier when you smile."

That took me by surprise, I can tell you.

Monday

Cat and I have made it up. May the best man win and all that, well, girl in this case. If I'm honest, I think Wes would have driven me mad as he's not really that bright at all and I know I don't suffer fools well, never have. Don't get me wrong he's not stupid. He's a lovely fellow, kind and gentle but he is a bit slow and pondering. The four of us (that includes Andrew) were playing cards together, which is something I find boring as I can remember all the cards as they fall, but Wes

176

was painfully slow to catch on at times. I shan't do that again in a hurry.

Andrew, on the other hand, well…... You could never call him slow or pondering. He's incredibly intelligent and an absolute whiz at maths and science, but particularly maths. He showed me his books on various theorems. Some are quite old written a hundred years ago, even more. His e-reader, too, is full of them, unlike mine which is all novels. But we have a good rapport and get on well. He does like art, so we thought we'd go to the galleries when we get back. He thinks art, music and maths are all closely related. Can't see it myself, but who knows?

Tuesday

Again here I sit with my e-Tec. I like writing and have always kept a diary. Not everyday perhaps, but usually made a note of anything interesting that happened. Strangely there is a gap between the end of April and the beginning of June. Six weeks is a long time for me to miss and I can't believe my life was that boring.

This last week seems to be going so fast. Only four more days to go. It'll be nice to see mum again. I've missed her while we've been away. Do you know, I can't even remember where we've been or why, for that matter? That's why I went back to check my diary for clues. Ah well, I expect it was a boring school trip or something. So educational that I've already forgotten it.

Later

I was reading through some of my old stories and came across something very strange. I must have written it, but it's nonsense in the middle of a perfectly ordinary sentence. It was a story about actors taking part in a play. We'd been doing a study on Shakespeare and that was probably what inspired me. I am becoming sidetracked, sorry. In the middle of this long narrative bit, quite out of the blue, is 'I hate the name Ophelia; change vowels for numbers'. Then the sentence continued as if nothing was out of the ordinary. At first I deleted it, but changed my mind and said undo. The one idea I have had is that it is a password to some document or other, but when I typed it in nothing happened. Mind you I may have got the numbers wrong. I can't be bothered to delve into it now so I'll leave it, the mystery may solve itself.

Wednesday

I am making up for lost time! Three diary days in a row, must be a record!

Andrew is a good friend and a nice person to know. A good mate to have on your side in a difficult situation. Don't ask me how I know, I just do. He can be abrupt at times but at least he doesn't mess around with great excuses or explanations. He has a very quick mind.

Over the last two days we've got to know each other. We've talked a lot about our families and childhood. His Mum is a very dominant character like mine. She is a well known mathematician. He told me his middle name, Euclid, after an ancient Greek mathematician; something to do with geometry, apparently. He said he doesn't know his Dad very well; he is away a lot. I can understand this a bit as my Dad left when I was four. I wish I'd had the chance to get to know him.

The one thing he did do is give me the name Ophelia! That's how I know the message in that story was written by me, as I really hate the name. So it must have been something important for me to have written it there. Andrew was surprised when I told him my real name. A sort of conspiratorial secret.

"But you're known as Jay?"

"My middle name is Jacaranda. Mum's a botanist."

"Ah." We both rolled our eyes, and agreed to keep schtum. "Parents! He said, "Who'd 'ave em!"

I like Andrew. Romantically? Perhaps, who knows what the future holds? But he's fun to be with and plays a mean game of chess, and I have won, fairly, on a few occasions. There are other games as well, where we're more equally matched. I'm glad we got together, it's good to have someone to talk to. Cat is so often at her piano now, with Wes humming along.

I've never heard some of the music she plays before, maybe she writes her own. I must remember to ask her about it. Sometimes it reminds me of the twenty-first century painters. Their unique style, with splodges of colour on an otherwise bland canvas. A bit like the sudden appearance of nebulae as we travel through space. Why I should think of paintings when listening to music is beyond me. Maybe Andrew's theory about art, music and maths is true. I wonder if he sees equations in his mind when listening to Cat?

The focus now from the observation point, is Mars. Something you don't see when living there as life is spent in the city bubble. You can see why it's called the red planet.

Friday

Our last day on the Temeraire. Tomorrow we will be home again. I expect Mum will be waiting to meet me. Maybe Andrew's parents will be there too, we could introduce them. You never know, they might get on.

I didn't write yesterday as it was a day much as the one before and probably this one will be as well. Time now to get up and dressed for first pill. At least these conversation times have become less boring, perhaps because we are nearing the end of our long journey.

Oh heck! I'm now all of a tizz! They announced after pill that we will dock at midday today. A full twenty four hours early. I hope Mum will be there. But now I must get all my stuff together and packed up.

Later

Big panic! I dropped my e-Tec. It bounced on the floor and I thought I'd smashed it. Luckily it was only the cover which has split. It's very old and tatty, I wonder why I didn't replace it when I got my new e-Tec, although that was some time ago and the cover was OK then. With my fingers crossed, I turned it on to check and all is fine.

At last everything is packed. Andrew arrived to collect my bag for me. (Isn't that sweet of him?) As we went out he almost trod on a very small Mem-Tic, certainly the smallest I've ever seen, though he went on about how they could be microscopic dots. Anyway, I wrapped it in a tissue and put it in my pocket. Thought no more about it as we sat with the others waiting to dock.

There wasn't time for a last game of chess and we'd already swapped communication details, so we sat chatting, remembering silly incidents etc. Even Del was amiable. We've all lived so closely together for such a long time. Sad goodbye's I think.

Mum was waiting for me. It was a tearful reunion. Andrew's parents were there, his Mum was in tears as well, but we did introduce them. His Dad, an older version of Andrew, looked very strangely at us. It was a look I didn't understand, but he seemed nice enough, they both did.

Now I am home, in my own bed, having spent the evening with Mum.

28

Revelations

Monday 30th July 2265

I am so bored!

Mum is back at work today and I can't settle to anything. I wish the others were here. Andrew, Cat, even the dreaded Delman to argue with would be better than this.

Mem-Tic! Of course, the perfect time to see what it's all about. I found it in the washing basket. I guess it fell out of my pocket. When I connected it encrypted nonsense came up on screen. What next? I thought for a moment and laughed as it dawned on me. I hate the name Ophelia! So this is where it comes in.

I tried '3h1t2th2n1m34ph2l31, nothing. Then, '3H1T2TH2N1M34PH2L31', still nothing. Then I switched it round with 'a' being 5 instead of 1. Eureka! A whole bunch of hidden files, eleven in all.

I opened the first one. It is all about a journey to Earth. As I started reading I realised it was the missing period of my diary- well, not all as it began about 10th May and ended on 23rd, but it might explain what had happened.

I read the first five files, by which time I was shaking, or shivering as I had gone very cold. I wasn't sure I wanted to read any more. I drank a glass of water and phoned Andrew, this involved him as much as me.

"Hi," he answered cheerily as he activated the viewer. "I was just thinking about you and won...... Jay, what's the matter? What's happened?"

"Are you alone?"

"Yep! What is it? You look awful."

"You remember that tiny memory device you nearly trod on, well, I'm beginning to wish you had. I found the password and opened it. You need to read this. How soon can you get here? I'd say meet halfway but I'm a bit too shaky."

"Twenty minutes, thirty tops. What's your Mars Mono Rail station? Janos?"

"Yes."

"Get a cold drink and sit down. If you feel faint put your head between your knees. I'll keep in contact. Leaving now."

So I sat down and waited. I was calmer now, knowing he was on his way, and decided to read on. He sent messages as promised, so when he arrived I was ready for him with the door open. I burst into tears.

He hugged me and then sat next to me on the sofa.

"You're not going to believe this,"I said miserably. I'm not sure I do. Here." I handed him my e-Tec. He gazed at my worried expression. "I've read up to the end of May 20th. Maybe we could read it together from there. You'll see what I mean as you read."

I sat, looking at him, watching his expressions change as he read. He was as intrigued as I had been. He was a quick reader and it didn't take him long to get to the end of the sixth file. By then the colour had drained from his face and he looked stunned.

"Where did you find this?" he asked. "No that's

not exactly what I mean. Has it always been on your e-Tec? Why haven't you mentioned it before?"

"Yes, well no! Let me explain. You remember when you picked up the Mem-Tic? It was on that. I must have hidden it in the old cover of my e-Tec. Why or when it was put there who knows, but when I dropped it the cover split and it must have fallen out. Here, if you look carefully under the clasp there is a tiny cavity. That must have been the hiding place."

"But why go to all that trouble? Although it's definitely about us and the others on the Temeraire. Jay, I think we should read the rest and see what's going on."

Carefully we read on. Slower this time, to be sure of taking in every word. For a long while after we sat together in silence. Andrew put his arm round me, a gesture of solidarity perhaps.

"That's why I didn't recognise the music Cat was playing – it was colour music, apparently originally mine. This is all so unbelievable. We know all seven of us were 'normal' for want of a better word. But this talks about disabilities, me being deaf and us signing."

"It means something else, too, Jay. It means we are clones."

29

Conversation with Otto

Monday 30th July 2265 – continued

"What exactly does that mean? Are we not real people? I feel like a real person. My monthly cycle is still the same. Surely, if I was a clone that wouldn't happen."

I knew I'd embarrassed him, but at that moment it was immaterial. What did it mean to be a clone?

Andrew shook off his unease and looked thoughtful. "You realise what we've discovered is absolute dynamite."

"I'm not sure I follow."

"Come on Jay, course you do. The Temeraire is a Termination Vessel. Anyone old or different is sent there to be destroyed or replaced by cloning. According to Mac, he and both our fathers are in some kind of clandestine plot where they hope to expose what the Guardians are doing to the people on Mars. I presume Mac and James are still on Earth, but Dad's here. I think we should contact him. When will your Mum be home?"

"Not for hours yet. She has some sort of meeting later, which will go on till about six."

Andrew speed dialled his Dad, I wondered what he was going to say. "Hi. I'm at Jay's. Something important's come up. We need your help. Can you come over here?"

Mr Rawlings arrived half an hour later. With that same no nonsense attitude as Andrew he said, "What's happened? How can I help?"

Andrew looked at me to lead the way. OK, I thought, how do I begin? "I have always written a diary and couldn't understand why there was so much missing- a whole six weeks. Then, when I was packing on the Temeraire….." Oh dear! This is so long winded. I started again, "I've discovered my missing diary and we've found out what went on on the Temeraire."

"Ah."

Andrew was bursting at the seems. "Is that all you can say, Ah?" You *knew* about all this! You developed the machine that vaporises anything, kills people! How *could* you? How can you live with yourself? How can you stand there so, so brazen and not be totally ashamed?"

"How much detail the diary goes into I am not sure, but there is something that I need to tell you both. The people I work for, that is the World Guardians of Peace, can be denied nothing. They rule the world. When I was ordered to develop the vaporiser I did it under great duress. I had no alternative. If not me someone else would have done it. This invention was, and still is top secret. Believe me your abhorrence of it is nothing in comparison to mine. Since its inception I've realised its planned use and have done my best to sabotage or destroy it but to no avail. This machine was illegally discussed with James and Mac and we decided that somehow the Guardians had to be stopped."

"But Mac says about us being the ones who will

inform on the Guardians. Why us? How are we involved?" Andrew had calmed down a bit now, but was still demanding.

"Jay, do you know about your colour music gift?" I nodded wondering what on earth that had to do with it. Then, as I thought back to the diary it dawned on me. I kept quiet and let Mr Rawlings continue. He would probably explain it better than me.

"You were unique. The only person in the world, or both worlds, who could ever have discovered that the Temeraire never left Mars orbit."

"I remember reading about that and losing my temper because you hadn't told me before, Jay." Andrew was still puzzled. "But how can we do the informing?"

"Not you, your original selves." He paused to let that statement sink in. "They are the only survivors of the Temeraire. There will never be any others and they have a tough assignment ahead."

He continued, slowly as if having to think carefully and be sure of the right words. I could understand that. "At the moment they are living in Paris, with friends, who are trying to find ways to expose the dreadful things the Guardians have in mind for the future of the World. You can be sure that the use of the Vaporiser on the Temeraire is a precursor to the use of it on Earth." Again another thoughtful pause.

"That diary contains vital information, Jay. Look after it carefully and keep it protected from discovery by anyone, even your mother. It may be needed to help bring the Guardians to justice. Most important to remember is that on no account must you be tempted to change any of it. Not a correction of any kind- not even a full stop. These files must remain identical to the ones on Earth. I cannot stress this enough.   You may be needed to help in some other way not yet thought of, but believe me, if you are needed your co-operation will be vital."

"Of course we'll help in any way we can. But how can we be normal now we know we are clones, not people in our own right?" I was thinking about Mum and how I should behave with her. "I will be living a lie. We both will. How can we act normally?"

"I know it's very difficult for you to take in everything. It might be a good idea to re-read the diary and get all the facts straight in your minds." He looked from one of us to the other and then said thoughtfully, after a long pause:"Would it help if I could organise another trip for you?"

"What do you mean? We've only just returned from Earth." Andrew was more himself now, and intrigued. I was too.

"The Endeavour leaves for Jupiter in two days time. If I could get you on that, it would give you time, more chance to understand everything that's gone on. Time together, away from enquiring mothers."

"I shall be travelling with you, so your mother, Jay can rest assured that I'll look after you."

"Jupiter! Wow!" Andrew's excitement was obvious, I wasn't so sure. I mean Mum had been on her own for three months already. I didn't think she'd be very enthusiastic. Maybe she could get together with Andrew's mum, be company for each other.

"I don't know. I'll need to talk it through with Mum," I said doubtfully. But there was an inkling of the adventurous spirit there as well.

"I can't make promises, but if I am to do this I need to leave now and get things organised. Andrew, stay here with Jay, don't be too late home. Talk about everything, and remember Jupiter is an exciting planet."

We sat there for ages, talking about the diary. Trying to work out what it meant to be a clone. What were the restrictions on our lives? Would we be able to have children?

I asked Andrew this question and then realised what I'd said. "I don't mean together or anything, I only mean would we be, you know, *normal*?"

Off handed he replied, "I quite liked that idea." and then changed the subject back to the reading of the diary. I handed my e-Tec to him.

"Here, I can remember it almost word for word." He was disbelieving until I told him to open the entry for May 20th and then started to recite it for him.

He sat, open mouthed, looking particularly stupid. "It's just one of those strange phenomena. A bit like your maths thing – mine's English. I think it's known as total recall, but I'm not sure. Mind you I've never tried it with another language. Then I've never learnt another language. Why bother when the whole of Mars speaks English. I wonder how I'd get on if it was in Russian or Chinese? But then I'd have to find something written in…….."

"Jay? Will you please be quiet? I am *trying* to concentrate."

30

Anthony Rawlings (Otto)

Monday, July 30th 2265

It felt strange to be imparting the same information to the two of them as I had done on the Endeavour with Carli and John. At least it was easier now to think of Andrew as John. It was the only way to differentiate between them.

Otto was reflecting as he travelled back to his office. He too was scheming and planning and he didn't think that the kids would be pleased when they found out. But it was essential that they and their mothers believed him now.

Once there he wasted no time in contacting James. The call automatically diverted to the house.

"Otto," answered James, "Good to hear from you. How's life back on Mars? More to the point how are things with you and Andrew?"

"That is why I need to speak to you. I had an interesting conversation with both of them. It is an uncanny feeling to be talking with my son and yet not. The crucial point is that the missing part of Jay's diary has been found, and read. The revelations from it caused a rumpus I can tell you. I will not go into detail. Clever girl you've got there, James. Her quick thinking has given me an idea."

"Takes after her father!"

"I shall ignore that. The idea of them being clones has shocked them to the core. They are nervous of having to keep it secret from family. Plus the information about the Temeraire. I have suggested a trip to give them time to get used to the idea and to find out what being a clone really means. I can't help them with this. Might get some info from Mac, but I doubt it. But it will give me a chance to find out what I can for them."

"You mean, put them back on a ship to Earth? Doubt if they'll be keen."

"Not if I tell them, as I have, that they will be going to Jupiter."

"Otto, you can't do that to them. It's the sort of underhand trick Mac would use!"

"I am aware of that, and I don't like it, but it's important that no-one knows they are on their way back to Earth. Especially not Mac. Not even Carli or John for the moment. Luckily both Discovery and Endeavour leave on the same day, almost the same time."

"I wouldn't like to be around when you tell them."

"James! Will you stop this pettiness! No wonder Mac loses his temper with you. It's too good a chance to miss. When they have re-read the diary and are more familiar with the content and its implications, I think they will understand."

"Now if that is all, I shall call them at Jay's and let them have the good news." Then, almost as an afterthought, "How are your two faring?"

"Well. They are away for a few days with Elise's parents. Extended family visiting. Have you read the diary? I have and am currently persuading my publisher to take it on. Ostensibly as a work of fiction. I should hear from them soon. I may have difficulty persuading them not to edit anything. Then it's all systems go with the media."

"We're due into Florida 29th August. Can you organise continuation flights for us. Don't want to get that far and find out everything's booked. Likewise can you arrange a family hotel suite. First or Second Airport hotels, either is fine."

"Will do. That timing is good, more or less what we were working on. Need to go. Over and out."

"James can be infuriating, but he does have contacts," muttered Otto as he rang Andrew's number.

"Hello, son. How's things?"

"OK. We've been talking and one thing Jay wants to do is meet her father. Do we have to go Jupiter? I checked and there is another ship, the Discovery leaving at nearly the same time. It's going to Earth. Any chance we could get on that instead?"

Surprised, and more than a little relieved, Otto replied. "Ah. Just arranged your passage on the Endeavour with me. Can't change now. Sorry. I thought you were enthusiastic about Jupiter?"

This wasn't his Andrew who was single minded and could be very selfish. He's putting the girl first. Had to grow up sometime I guess. She's a smart kid. He could do a lot worse. But then, he's not my son is he?

"Dad! You still there?" Andrew heard a grunt from the other end. "Jay's OK with that. It was only a whim, after all."

"If there are any problems, tell Jay to get her mother to call me. See you later." Abruptly he ended the call. There was a lot to do including a bit of roguery, just to help things along.

Irritably he answered the phone which spoiled his train of thought. "Rawlings!" he bellowed.

"Otto. Good news. They have agreed to publish the diary, warts and all. No editing whatsoever. What's even better is that they want it in hard copy. Apparently there has been a resurgence in good old fashioned books. Started in May after we left. It has become trendy with teenagers to own books, the latest must have craze. They are marketing Jay's diary as a work of teenage fiction under the title of 'Life on Mars'. She will be so pleased."

"When?"

"What do you mean, when?"

"When will it go to press?" Oh, James, come on keep up with me, he thought.

"They start in two weeks. With the launch at the end of August. Perfect timing for the August programme of 'Is This Rubbish?'on the 31st. I've met the producer a couple of times and am sure I can get him to discuss the book and interview Carli. With any luck this could be their 'Book of the Month.' Hey presto! Mission accomplished!"

"Good news indeed, more than we could ever have imagined. Well done. Have you said anything to Mac yet?"

"No, I haven't been able to locate him, vanished into thin air. When you consider that it was his idea in the first place he's kept a remarkably low profile through all this. Even on the Endeavour he was absent most of the time. What's going on inside that brain of his? I know Carli's got no confidence in him and, quite honestly I'm beginning to have doubts myself."

"So am I, James, so am I. If you agree, I think we should keep this between ourselves for now, apart from the kids, of course, though I shall say nothing to my pair until we are safely on the Discovery. There will be no opposition to their being taken to Earth, by the way. Apparently Jay wants to meet you and was disappointed when I'd booked the trip to Jupiter. No, my biggest problem is keeping them in our cabin for the duration."

"Carli and John will be back tomorrow so I shall tell them about the book then. Elise is home now with the twins. Thanks to your space station we are thinking of giving them a bigger play room. Just thought you'd like to know. Must go, over and out."

31

Mum has a problem

Tuesday, 31st July

"ABSOLUTELY NOT!" This was Mum's reaction to my suggestion about the trip to Jupiter. "You have been away for three months. I have been so looking forward to your return. I have vacation booked from Wednesday for a month so we can be together."

I tried to hide my disappointment, tried hard not to cry. But I knew my Mum, if her mind was made up there was no changing it, I didn't even try.

I sloped off to my room and called Andrew.

"Ah," he said, "Umm. Wait and see." Then he hung up on me! The rat!

As we watched the TV Mum went on to explain about all the things she had planned for us to do. I feigned enthusiasm and tried not to let it get me down. In the end I went to bed early to read. It took a long while to get to sleep.

I was woken by the shrill ringing of the house phone, we both were. It was five in the morning – was something wrong?

I heard this end of the call, I couldn't miss it. Mum was yelling into the instrument. I pitied the poor person on the other end. 'Don't shoot the messenger' went through my brain. When she put the receiver down I handed her a glass of cold water.

"What's happened?"

"You may well ask. Some idiot, some incompetent nincompoop has completely messed up!" She almost spat this at me. "All the work I've done over the last three months has been lost, obliterated. All of it. Everything. And more. My previous experiments, lab work, everything gone."

"But, Mum, I thought you were some sort of program designer?"

"Yes, but I've been working on vegetable production experiments while you were away. They want to introduce food back on Mars. Make us self sufficient in vegetable production as the original intentions were a few decades ago. An important project. I have been working on it night and day while you were away. It was perfect for me to be so involved."

"But how was it all lost?" Mum was so distraught, I felt so sorry for her.

"Some electrical fault apparently. Everything got sprayed with the wrong chemicals, herbicide, would you believe? Even my terminal was sprayed. Probably wiped out all my data"

"Recoverable?" I asked hopefully.

"Of course, but it will take time. All the planting and lab work will need redoing and my assistant has transferred to another project. No, I have to resign myself to repeating it all. At least this time I'll know how to proceed, rather than all the previous guesswork."

"Jay, I'm sorry. This is going to be a very boring time for you for the next two months or even more."

"Oh Mum, don't worry. Is there any way I can help?"

"Sweet of you to ask, love, but no. It's all too specialised." Then, as if she had a sudden thought, "Do you still fancy going to Jupiter? You may as well go now. There won't be much for you here."

"If you're sure, I'll call Andrew and see if I can change my mind."

I'd forgotten the time and speed dialled before I remembered it was five thirty am. He answered immediately, almost as if he had been waiting for my call.

"Morning, Jay. What's new?" He was smiling.

"There's been a problem at Mum's work and she's going to have to work long hours over the next couple of months repeating stuff. But it does mean that I can go with you to Jupiter if it's not too late."

"See, I told you to wait. You never know what's going to happen." His voice sounded odd. There was no surprise or relief there. I tried to work it out. "I'll see you at ten." I was still wondering when he ended the call. Typical Andrew, he hadn't even said where.

I was sorting through what I wanted to take with me when both he and his father arrived. It was only eight. At least I was dressed, I thought, but they could have let me know.

"Great news, Jay. I'm glad you can make it. Now, I don't have a lot of time and I need to ask you something." His Dad was looking very serious.

"OK," I said, wondering what it was about.

"Do you have any proof of your colour music abilities?"

"Seeing that I have absolutely no recollection of it,

I doubt it very much. Is it important?"

Andrew added, "The more proof we have the better. This would really help, Jay" They had obviously been discussing things in my absence.

"Mr Rawlings, I do know there are some tapes of me as a small child." Andrew turned his attention to the collection of DVD's etc on the shelf. "No, not there, I think they're on an old camera. It'll be in the box at the back of the hall closet." Almost before I'd finished speaking he'd collected the box and brought it into the living room. "I don't even know why we've still got it. You're supposed to hand equipment like cameras back to get the new one."

"Is there anything else you can think of that might be of use? Oh, and please do call me Otto, no use for formality if we are all to be travelling together."

"There's nothing here, I'm sure, but there is the film," suddenly remembering an event on the Temeraire."Maybe we could borrow that?"

"Film?" He asked.

"Yes. But it's not of me. Wes wanted something to do on the voyage and he was messing around with an old movie camera we found. You'd be surprised the stuff that turned up in the cubbyholes of that ship. Oops, sorry. He made tapes of us all. Then he made a film of Catalina playing. The music was strange, haunting. It was like nothing I'd ever heard before so I asked her about it. She explained that it was in her head. At the time she was watching a beautiful colourful display in space. I'll call her and ask if we can borrow it." I went to my bedroom to do this.

"Dad, can we take Catalina with us? Then she can demonstrate it to everyone."

"No. If we can use the film that will be adequate. Besides it too late to arrange another little power mishap, and I don't think her parents would take kindly to their daughter being whisked away so soon.

I returned from phoning. "She hasn't got it, Wesley has, but she's sure he wouldn't mind. I didn't say we'd need it for two months or so. Is there any way it could be copied and then returned?"

"Not a problem, thank you for phoning her. Will she call Wesley?"

"She gave me his number. I'll call now." Which I did. He was pleased to hear from me and I thought it rude to cut all the preliminaries. But eventually I asked about the film and he was fine about lending it. He offered to bring it here, but I had a sudden brainwave and I asked him if he could get to Otto's office instead, knowing how central it was, and that he lived the far side of town. He agreed, said it was much easier and arranged to meet us in half an hour.

Wes was delighted to see us and we sat and chatted while Otto had the film copied. As easy as that. I left the boys talking, while I went home to pack. Then I remembered that I'd promised to check what was on the old camera and spent a fun hour going through it all. Some of it would be useful I am sure. I tucked it into my bag.

All this is a long winded way of recording what went on this morning. I tell you, by noon I was drained. I'm excited about tomorrow and looking forward to the trip.

32

Back on a Starship

Wednesday August 1st 2265

Mum came to Andrew's with me. She'd met the Rawlings' and I was glad she'd wanted to accompany me. I hoped she and Elizabeth would get on together and be company for each other while we were all away.

We were both greeted as old friends and before long they were Liz and Jenny. That's good, I thought.

We talked about the trip, but, as we had an air-trans to catch and the Mum's had to get to work, it wasn't for long. Goodbye's said, we were on our way.

"We've got a secret!" Andrew said in a silly sing-song voice and a silly grin on his face. "You'll be pleased!" Otto, on the other hand, glowered at his son.

I gave up trying to second guess what he was on about, but a sudden image of Earth came into my head. He was still grinning like a Cheshire Cat. I thought about the cat from the old book and the famous story. To think it had lasted over three hundred years. I wonder if I could ever write something that would last for three years, let alone three hundred………

"Jay!" Andrew had shouted at me. "Did you remember your e-Tec?" They were both looking anxiously at me. Secrets? I'll teach them, I thought. I stared wide eyed, took a quick, sharp intake of breath and put my hand to my mouth. Then I gave it away with my eyes sparkling mischievously.

"You'll give me a heart attack if you do that again." Otto smiled as he said it but I knew he was serious and I was sorry, but only a bit.

We arrived at the terminal and made our way to the shuttle. We were early as the Endeavour wasn't due to leave until late this afternoon and there were only two others waiting. It didn't seem to matter. As soon as we were aboard, luggage stashed, the craft set off for the space terminus. It didn't take long. Travelator to the appropriate departure gate and we were welcomed aboard – the USS Discovery!

"The secret!" beamed Andrew. "We're going to Earth!"

Otto led the way. He knew exactly where we were going and which cabin was ours. "Here we are." He keyed in the entry code and the door opened to reveal a very nicely appointed sitting room with furniture like I'd never seen before. There was a colourful rug, a sofa and some cushions spread around; very home like, but nicer than anything on Mars. There were two separate bedrooms, both with their own bathroom and the larger one had another smaller room off it. There was a baby crib in here as well as a single bed. The closets were all built into the walls. There was attractive, voice controlled, lighting.

"Andrew, give me a hand." He grabbed the cot, "we'll put this in the main cabin, give you more room." He'd already deposited Andrew's bags on the floor. My things had been left in the other, slightly smaller cabin.

"Family accommodation." he said. "I thought it would be best if we were all together. Apologies for the deception, but it has become important for you both to be on Earth, without anyone knowing. Andrew thought you'd be OK with it, Jay."

I was still shocked, but as I thought about it the prospects of seeing Earth definitely outweighed a trip to Jupiter. "Yes, yes of course." Would we meet my father? My mind was going wild, maybe we'd meet our original selves. My attention was drawn back to Otto and what he was saying.

"It is essential that no-one knows that you two are on this ship. For that reason it will be necessary for you to stay in our quarters. I am sorry about this but it is of primary importance. I should not insist otherwise."

"There is, however, one saving grace." He went over to the far wall and drew apart the drapes to reveal our own private view of the universe. I stared into space.

"It won't be so bad. Like being on the Temeraire, without Delman our major pain in the bum. We'll be fine, really we will."

I wasn't so sure. Being cooped up together for four weeks in one small space was not my idea of fun. I wish I had Andrew's optimism.

"You will have access to the ship's online library. And there are various games here. I can get more for you. The alternative is to put you into an induced coma, but that does carry risks and should be done in the Medical Centre rather than here. If you can cope on your own it will be much better."

He went through to Andrew's cabin and opened one of the drawers, revealing colourful clothing! "I came aboard earlier and have arranged several changes of clothes for you both. I had help with sizes and colours so I hope you will both enjoy wearing something different. Brighten up the journey. Also to hide your presence, Mars uniform must not be sent to the laundry. Keep it for when we land, you may need it at the end of the month."

I resisted the urge to ask who helped, as I was keen to see what had been organized for me. This was a whole new experience! Colour! I was miles away. I wondered how he'd found the right sizes, but answered my own question. Of course, The Ministry of Citizenship. I was miles away.

"Jay. You look a little disconcerted. Are you OK with all this?" Otto was peering anxiously at me.

"Of course, I'll be fine. I don't mean to be anti. It's all so new, different, exciting. The surprise of everything, change of plan, you know." And I think he did understand. It must have been difficult for Otto to arrange all this, especially for us to have portholes. Large though they are, I think technically they are still called portholes.

"I can always tie you to a chair if you get too frisky!"

"*Andrew*!"

He was obviously in some sort of stupid childish mood. I gave in and laughed. May as well enjoy each other's company. Maybe I could write a book?

33

The book

Wednesday August 1st 2265

We arrived back home later last night than expected. We had a lovely trip with Henri and Françoise. We did a tour of 'the Rellies' as Papa called them. They all seemed delighted to meet us and weren't in the least bothered that I was James' older daughter. A shoulder shrug or a 'ça va' was the order of the day. I had been swatting up on Australia, but I needn't have bothered. No-one asked where I'd lived, just accepted that I was with my mother. I was glad I hadn't had to lie to them.

We were travelling in the area of Reims and Henri took us to meet an old friend whose family's vineyard has been producing Champagne for hundreds of years. I love Champagne, although with the first sip the bubbles always go down my nose. Andrew thinks it's a girlie drink and would rather have beer – philistine.

What fantastic news about the book! I hadn't dared to hope that it would really be published. As a proper book too, in only four weeks time. I'm not sure I know what a teenage craze is, but long may it last. This is my dream come true. Today we are meeting the publisher and I have to decide on the cover. I think it has to be a photo of Mars from space, glowing all red.

"Carli, Carli, where are you?"
That's Andrew. It must be time to go.

Later

The meeting went well. I was nervous at first and I couldn't believe what they were saying about my book. They seem to think I have an amazing imagination – if only they knew. But Papa says I must not even hint that it could be a true story. Andrew thinks this is rather a shame. because when it's revealed as true on the programme then the sales are bound to go up and they'll have to reprint it instead of having enough copies in the first place. Typical Andrew logic but he does have a point.

They agreed about the dust cover picture and even had two ready for me to choose from, one of which was perfect. I can't believe how enthusiastic they are. Then they wanted biographical detail for the inside back cover. Thank goodness Papa was ready with something he'd written and it seemed to satisfy them. I heaved a sigh of relief. I should never have known what to say if he hadn't been there.

34

Anthony Rawlings

Tuesday August 28th 2265

"Cavendish?"

Otto's use of James' surname immediately told him to be aware that it was not a secure line.

"Good morning Otto, how may I be of assistance?"

"As you know we arrive tomorrow, and I was wondering which flight we are booked on?"

"The twelve noon to New York and the trans-Atlantic supersonic from there the following morning. Overnight at The First Hotel. Collect tickets at the airport for both flights. You should be in Paris for breakfast."

"Good. Thank you for that. How are things your end?"

"I'm not sure. I'm hoping we're not going to have a problem."

"You mean with the book?"

"No, that's almost ready for distribution. My problem is with Carli and John. They've disappeared."

"What do you mean 'disappeared'?"

"Mac arrived two days ago and took them off. I'm beginning to get worried."

"Why? Did he not say how long they would be

away?"

"No. All he said was that he wanted to them to meet someone in Paris. They have nothing with them, not even a change of clothes."

"I don't like this, James. Does he have any idea about the book or the TV programme?"

"As far as I know, none whatsoever. He has had no dealings with my publishers and I asked them to keep the book within closed doors. They will want to do that anyway, for fear of being upstaged by another publisher, especially as it's so close to the show. There's always a lot of rivalry for the top spot."

"Can the launch go ahead without Carli?"

"It can, but then there would be no evidence about the truth of the story, and ruin the whole purpose of the event. It might not be a complete disaster but not far from it."

"Have you any idea what could be in Mac's mind? Where he would take them? I thought he was as keen on our plan as we are, it was his idea in the first place."

Otto was quiet for a moment. "Do you know how well in he is with those in Geneva? I told you I saw him at the airport when I was there in June."

"Can he have changed his mind?"

"Possible", Otto replied, I know he has a very close relationship with them. He is their main man on the other ship." He was very much aware of the vulnerability of this line's security and chose his words with care. "James, the kids could be in danger. Keep me informed? You have my Satfone details and I should be within communication distance this evening. Over and out."

35

Arrival

Tuesday August 28th 2265

    I can't believe its four weeks since we left Mars. Otto says we will dock early tomorrow. He needs us to be ready by seven, in our new clothes so we will blend in with everyone else, and he's given us another larger bag each so we can pack everything in together.

    I haven't written my diary during the trip. I thought it would be very dull and repetitive. The days have been the same, but that doesn't mean not enjoyable. We get on well together, in fact I really can't imagine being without Andrew now. We seem to know what each other are thinking, almost like two halves of a whole, if you see what I mean.

    I'm not infatuated with him or anything, he's just, well, Andrew! And I've got better at chess. He'll still wins often but I'm a good match for him now.

    Oh dear I am going on about nothing, so I'll stop and continue when there's something to report.

Later

    We were closing the 3D chess game as Otto returned. I think he's been working with someone he knew in one of the labs. He wasn't away all the time but most mornings.

He sat down and gave us a very headmasterly sort of look. "I need to talk to you about something."

Oh heck, I thought I don't *think* we've done anything wrong. I hope he's not going to give us an embarrassing lecture on the birds and bees. Surely the time for that was four weeks ago; not that we've even thought about anything in the least bit romantic.......

"Jay, you off on one again?" As usual I was brought to reality by Andrew.

"Dad's trying to ask us about food."

"Food? I thought it was going to be....... Ah, um, yes, food?"

"Yes. So far you've only ever eaten your pills and drunk water. Your metabolism is designed, for want of a better word, for this, rather than proper food. There is a very minor operation that can be performed to adjust your digestive tract to take normal meals. I have organised an opportunity for this procedure to be carried out tonight, if you so desire. You should feel no ill effects and I assure you that there are no risks involved. But because you will only be on Earth for a short period you may feel it is unnecessary. I do have a large supply of your normal pills with me if they are required."

"Advantages?" Andrew had voiced my question.

"You will be able to eat anything. A whole new experience for you. Eating in company is one of the great pleasures of life, especially as we shall be travelling on to Paris very soon; perhaps the food capital of the world."

"Disadvantages?"

"Oh, Andrew, surely even you can see that!" I

shocked myself and the others with my reply. "Oops, I'm sorry. Can I ask how you manage, Otto? You travel back and forth a lot, I think."

He looked a bit nonplussed. "My metabolism is adjusted. I do miss food when I'm back on Mars, though. That is your main drawback."

"I vote we go for it. There may never be another chance. Anyway people will think it odd if we don't eat." Andrew gave me his 'go for it girl' look.

"OK, why not?"

I thought back to what mum had said when she heard about her disaster at work. "Apparently they are wanting to introduce food back on Mars. That's what Mum was working on while we were away before. In fact she'll be doing the same again now, repeating all her work, because of some mishap."

"Ah, yes." Otto looked suddenly guilty.

No, I thought, he couldn't have – could he? I must remember to ask Andrew, he'll know.

Wednesday 29th

I'm really excited, our first visit to Earth. Otto woke us at three this morning and took us to a deserted Med Centre, apart from a very nice lieutenant who was to perform the operations. Thirty minutes later we were back here again. Don't know what the fuss was all about.

It's still early. We have arrived and will be disembarking very soon. I should have said how beautiful Earth is as we approached it. We've been watching it for three weeks now, slowly getting bigger until it filled the whole porthole. Oops. Got to dash.

Later

Otto handed us passports as we left. I'd completely forgotten that we would need official documents and I got a surprise when I opened it. It wasn't mine! The photo was me but the name was Carli Meredith Cavendish! Andrew's was for someone called John, John Rawlings.

On the shuttle he explained that he'd had to use printing facilities on board and the only documentation available was from our original selves, who now had new names as we had required their old ones back on Mars! All very confusing. He asked us to act the part and be Carli and John if anyone questioned us, which he was sure they wouldn't.

The arrival and all the necessary paperwork went smoothly and we made our way on the overhead monorail to the airport. We were booked on a flight to New York at ten, although we still arrived early and Otto found us a table in the café for some breakfast. Our first real food! He chose coffee and something he called doughnuts for us all. He showed us how to dunk them. They were delicious, ring shaped, with lovely crunchy sugar on the outside.

I've decided to try and use as many of these new words as I can remember, then I'll get used to them and they won't seem so odd. I wondered about spelling, but my e-Tec must know them as they haven't shown up with red lines under. We must get used to all these different foods, so we blend in with everyone.

I enjoyed the flight to New York. Some of the time we could see the coastline of America way below, although we mostly flew over the sea. I sat next to the window, though I did have to put up with Andrew leaning across me whenever there was anything to look at, especially when we came into land a couple of hours later. The flight steward told him to sit back and fasten his seat belt.

New York

New York is so Amazing! I love it especially in the late afternoon sun. Everywhere is so full of life. I could write a whole book about it. Maybe that's what I'll do. We have a wonderful view as we're on the eighteenth floor of our hotel. Perhaps we'll be able to stay here longer when we get back from Paris. I wonder why we are going to Paris?

There was the sound of a phone. Otto glanced at his but ignored it. A short while later he picked up the voice-mail and cursed aloud. He then went into another room and we could hear him talking to someone, but not clearly.

I'm looking forward to tomorrow, I'm sure it will be an exciting adventure.

36

Missing

Wednesday August 29th 2265

We have been kidnapped! I can't believe it. Mac lied to us when he said he wanted to take us to meet a colleague in Paris. Instead here we are on a small jet, flying heaven knows where. Papa and Elise must be frantic. It's three days since we left the house.

It all began so amicably. Mac arrived on Saturday afternoon. He even played football with Papa, Andrew and the boys. Henri and Françoise came over and Elise made a wonderful meal for everyone. Andrew insisted that we should clear away afterwards, and make the coffee. I don't know what conversation went on while we were in the kitchen, but I'm sure Papa and Elise aren't a part of this. No, I think it's Mac who's turned traitor.

It was Sunday morning when he asked us to go to with him to meet someone. I should have trusted my instincts and refused. I *so* wish I had. I've never liked the man, never trusted him. Papa thought it was a good idea and might be useful, so we went with him and ended up being thrown into a kind of dungeon, or cellar somewhere. It was certainly underground, cold and damp.

We had no idea where we were. He gagged us and

our hands and feet were tied with plastic straps. It was awful. Andrew managed somehow to get behind me so I could shift his gag down and he spat out the wad of stuff in his mouth. Then he grabbed my gag in his teeth and pulled it down for me. At least then I could breath properly. We tried yelling for help but no-one came. As I said we could have been anywhere. Mac returned three times with bread and cheese and some water, none of which was very fresh, but we were so desperate it didn't matter. He untied us while he was there and we both made fists when he retied our hands so we were able to get free. Leg ties were simple after that, making captivity so much easier.

Then this morning we were taken to a small, nearby airport. Straight through customs and onto a small private jet. I caught sight of a clock with the date otherwise I wouldn't even know how long we'd been locked up let alone what day it was. We have no watches or phones, of course. Now, above the Atlantic, we still have no idea what's going on.

Mac took our phones and my e-Tec so I have been scribbling like mad with my pen in my old notebook, thank goodness they were in my bag. But it's running out and soon I shall have to rely on memory alone.

"I think it's time for you to know what the future holds." Mac had been forward with the pilot and he was now standing in front of us. "You are en route to New York and thence to Florida and the Temeraire. You should never have been allowed to leave it. You will not return to Mars, your clones have replaced you. Your original fate awaits." He was smug, gloating. I hated him.

I looked at Andrew. You know what that means, I

thought. His own thoughts were more constructive. He told me not to despair, he had an idea. Not for the first time I thanked our lucky stars that Mac didn't know about our telepathy.

"But I thought you wanted us to expose the arrogance of the Guardians?" Andrew asked, trying to sound innocent and perplexed. What was he up to?

"Oh no, that is history. James and Otto will understand. A slight change of plan as I shall be joining The Guardians and becoming one of them. A most prestigious appointment. The youngest ever member. Therefore I cannot go against their beliefs and requirements. Besides old people have lived their lives, time to make room for the younger generation."

"You never did answer our question about what age life is terminated?"

What was Andrew doing? I didn't need to know any of this. All I could think about was the hopelessness of everything. Perhaps Papa would be able to launch the book for me. What a shame no-one would know what had happened to us. I wasn't listening to anything he was saying and, for once Andrew didn't take me to task.

"So Dad and James know nothing about your new appointment? What a shame. I'm sure they would have liked to congratulate you on your good fortune. As you say no-one over the age of 80 has the right to live at the expense of others. So what will happen about the cloning of children? You told us how costly that project is. Why not simply dispose of them at birth? I suppose it's difficult to detect blindness or deafness for that matter until the child is older."

"You are very astute. I could not have put it better myself."

I could not believe my ears! The two of them were casually chatting. Have you gone totally balmy, Andrew?

"Do you know, Mac, I'm really thirsty. Is there any chance of some coffee? I'd kill my Granny for a half decent drink."

"Coffee is available. I think I shall join you." He went to the back of the cabin. While his back was turned Andrew quickly signed, "Trying to get him relaxed and trust us to behave. We need him to drink lots so he has to leave us to use the toilet."

"You want some, Carli?" Mac called. There are sandwiches here as well.

I answered as unemotionally as I could, "Yes, thank you." Andrew was frantically nodding to me. He grabbed my notebook and the pencil but I couldn't see what he was writing. Mac turned and brought over our coffee.

The time dragged on. We had no idea how long this journey would take. Andrew was still talking to Mac and eventually I heard him ask how long the flight was and when we would arrive.

"Our ETA is fifteen forty five, local New York, about five hours. For some trivial reason we could not fly direct to Miami."

"I presume there is a toilet on board," I asked. Mac nodded and indicated the rear, near the kitchen area.

As I passed the coffee maker, on my way back, I refilled our mugs giving Mac the lion's share. He thanked me and started drinking without thought. What a shame I hadn't been able to poison it.

Andrew's plan worked as about half an hour later Mac made his way to the toilet and locked the door.

Andrew dashed forward to the cockpit with his note. Seconds later he returned. "Robots! Wretched robots," he said. "Robots flying the plane. Never thought of that, did I? Waste of a good plan. Have to think again now."

I suggested that he hand the note to the customs official. He nodded as Mac returned and they continued their inane conversation. This time I listened as Andrew cleverly directed him back to his favourite subject, well two really: cloning and MacKenzie. One highly intelligent scientist to another.

In a while he telepathically told me to write another note so we could both have one. I carefully wrote: 'We have been kidnapped. Please help us by calling my father Mr James Cavendish at the following Paris number- 0287 176 521197.' I presume Andrew's would have been similar, maybe with Otto's details on, but I couldn't remember those. All we could do now was keep our fingers crossed. I stretched out on the seats and went to sleep.

Ages later we had to fasten seatbelts as we were coming in to land.

In contrast to when we left, this airport was huge and very crowded. We never got a chance to pass our notes. Mac went straight through customs and immigration, flashing his official Guardians' ID. He handed over all three passports and we never got near enough to anyone. As we went through the arrivals area I caught a transmission from Andrew to pretend I was going to throw up.

"Jay, you OK?" he asked in all innocence. "You've gone a greenish colour."

I hid my face with my hand across my mouth and made a dash for the Ladies. I was wondering what to do next when a familiar face appeared from one of the cubicles. I couldn't believe my luck.

"Excuse me," I said hoping she would remember me. "It's Commander Johnson isn't it?"

I was never so pleased to hear her welcome accent. "Well, hello there. Carli I think. How are you two enjoying being on Earth?"

Now that was a strange thing to say. She wasn't supposed to know we'd escaped from Mars. Then a horrible thought struck me. How friendly was she with Mac? If I gave her the note would she take it straight over to him and dump me in it? I made my decision.

"Very much, thank you. Most of the time I'm living in Paris with my father and his lovely family. Looking forward to starting at the Sorbonne soon. John and I are here with Professor MacKenzie. They're waiting outside."

As she walked over to the hand drier she said, "I'll go say hi to them."

When she'd gone I stood there, not knowing what to do, tears rolled down my face, I sobbed in despair. An elderly lady came up to me.

"Are you all right, dear? Can I help you?" She said with a very cultured English accent, looking concerned. She found me a white, linen handkerchief.

"Thank you, you're very kind."

"Can I help at all," she asked. She was looking at me. Not unkindly but taking in my unkempt, dishevelled appearance. Four days in the same clothes had taken its toll and, embarrassed, I realised I probably didn't smell too good either.

"Only if you have a cell phone I can use. I need to contact my father. You see we've been missing for four days now and he will be frantic. It's a long story, but we were kidnapped and flown halfway round the world not knowing what was happening." It all came out between sobs.

"Well, dear, no I don't have my phone but my daughter has hers and I'm just on my way to meet her. Why don't you come too?"

"No, no, I can't be seen with anyone, but if I give you this number will you try and phone for me. If you could tell Papa I'm in New York, en route to the Temeraire, he will understand and know what to do. I should be so grateful, we both will. I know it sounds dramatic but please believe me when I say it really is a matter of life or death." I blew my nose again.

"You just leave it with me. I'll phone as soon as I can. Now, are you ready to face the world?" She had a lovely smile, which lit up her whole face, I put my trust in her.

We walked out together. Mac and Andrew were talking to Commander Johnson and to my horror she looked at us and said, "Mother, there you are."

My heart sank. It must have showed on my face because the old lady gave me a conspiratorial look and tapped the side of her nose with her index finger. I don't know what it meant but I had a feeling it was a sign that my secret was safe with her. Then she greeted her daughter and I knew she would keep her promise.

I think Andrew must have picked up some of this. He signed, tell me later.

While they talked he made a dive for the Gents, well timed as Mac could hardly dash off after him, without looking odd.

I caught some of the conversation and suddenly

realised that Commander Johnson's mum had found out where we'd come from, where we were staying and what flight we were on in the morning. She was fishing, doing an 'old lady inquisition' on him! What's more I was fairly sure that pompous ass Mac hadn't realised. Oh, thank you, thank you. Don't cry, I told myself, try not to get emotional.

Andrew returned looking pleased with himself. "I nicked someone's phone, he whispered."

"You WHAT?" I replied.

The others were chatting happily, so he whispered that he'd taken it from a man's back pocket as he knelt to tie his shoe lace. But it was turned off and he'd need the code to use it.

"So I handed it back. Said I found it on the floor and was it his? He was more than happy to let me try to call Dad. No luck, though I left a message. At least things are looking hopeful. What with you and the old lady?"

"She has Papa's number…...shush." Goodbyes were being said and Commander Johnson said how nice it was to see us again and to enjoy our holiday in Florida. Her mum took my hand and gave me a surprise hug, whispering "Good luck." as she did so.   "Thank you," was my hurried reply.

It was then back to the stern realities of bossy Mac. He ushered us to the exit and into a taxi. I overheard him ask for the Airport Sixth Hotel, where we were taken up to room 1485. I suppose it was all pre-booked because we had no interaction with reception staff.

As we went in the door, I seized my chance and grabbed the bathroom, locking myself in. The water was hot and wonderful. I wouldn't really have minded if it had been cold, I felt so dirty and disgusting. The hotel toiletries smelled nice. I put in the bath plug and dropped my underwear, top and socks into the warm water, trampling on them to help get them clean. My jeans I could live with, they would take longer to dry. The rest I would wear wet if I had to. Finally with my hair tied up in a large white towel and another round my body, I stood by the door and tried to transmit to Andrew that I was coming out and he needed to dash in after me. The childish side of me saw there were only two more towels and he must use both of them. Tough luck Mac.

37

James Cavendish

Wednesday August 29th 2265

"Hello. Am I speaking to Mr Cavendish? Mr James Cavendish?"

James was guarded, "Who is this?"

"No, I need to know first if I am speaking to the correct person."

She sounded an older lady, very English, very precise. "I am James Cavendish. How may I help you?"

"Ah, good. She was so upset you see and I had to be sure you were her father. You are Carli's father? I am Amelia Barrington-Smythe, by the way"

"Yes, yes. Have you seen her?"

"I met her in the Ladies about two hours ago and I have been trying to call you ever since. But my daughter seemed so familiar with that nasty man I had to wait until I was on my own. Finally I managed to persuade her that we should go to our hotel so that I could rest and change before dinner. So, while she is in the bath I have seized my opportunity."

"Yes, yes, thank you, but have you any news? Where is my daughter?"

"She said you would be worried. A bright spark, that one. I liked her enormously."

"Please, Mrs Barrington-Smythe, just tell me

where she is."

"Oh, didn't I say? We're in New York."

"No, not you, Madam, my daughter."

"Oh, she's here too. Look. I think I'd better start at the beginning, tell you what happened. I was in the Ladies room when I noticed this young lady, sobbing her heart out she was. She looked dishevelled, unkempt and she asked if she could use my phone………"

James listened patiently, hearing every detail of their meeting followed by all the information she had gleaned from Mac himself.

"Mrs Barrington-Smythe……."

"Oh, Amelia, please."

"Amelia, I don't know how to thank you. Carli and John disappeared last Sunday and my wife and I have been frantic with worry. One thing, how did you come to meet MacKenzie?"

"He's a colleague of my daughter, they were both on the same starship Endeavour. Mind you she doesn't think much of him. Oh as a doctor, yes, but as a person, ooh very different. These Australian expressions she comes out with sometimes, oh dear no. I don't think she liked him at all."

"Amelia, may I ask if you'd be willing to help them once again?"

"Of course, this is far more exciting than sightseeing!"

"First, may I have your hotel and room number?"

"First Airport Hotel, room 359. I never like to be too high, earthquakes, you understand, or is that San Francisco? The suite is in my daughter's name Commander Anita Johnson."

"Thank you, thank you so much. I must go now

and make another call, try to sort this mess out." As an afterthought he added, "You may get a call from someone called Rawlings, Anthony Rawlings. Thank you so much for your help. Goodbye."

"Goodbye, James and good luck."

"Good news, I hope." He hadn't realised that Elise was standing behind him.

"Well, at least now we know where they are, New York. I'll tell you all about Amelia when I've phoned Otto. Bear with me."

Intrigued, but relieved they had been found, Elise left him to it as James dialled Otto's Satfone. The line was busy so he redialled a few moments later. Otto answered on the first ring.

"Rawlings!"

"Otto. James. The kids have been found. Mac has them in New York, near the airport. They are currently at Sixth Hotel, no room number."

"I was trying to ring you. I stupidly missed a call from John as I didn't recognise the number. At least you've heard. Thank God for that!"

"Otto, Otto, don't ring off! You have an ally, an elderly lady in your hotel, Mrs Amelia Barrington-Smythe, room 359. She is expecting you to call her and she will help if she can. It was she who contacted me with the message from Carli."

"Well that's a bonus! I'll work out a plan and contact you later. Over and out."

James sank into a chair. Elise brought him coffee and he told her all about Amelia's meeting with Carli.

38

Anthony Rawlings

Wednesday 29thAugust 2265

An idea was forming, but first I needed to explain things to the others. "There has been a change of plan. We won't be able to go for a meal yet, and maybe not even tonight. You see John and Carli were kidnapped last Sunday and they are in New York, but not far away. I need to rescue them. I also need your co-operation."

"We're up for it!" This was Andrew, of course.

"I need you to pretend that you are the identical twins of Carli and John. Shortly we're going down to meet a very kind lady who's helping us. I want you to stay with her for a while."

"Fine. Let's go."

I rang through to room 359 and spoke to a Mrs Barrington-Smythe, who seemed to be expecting my call.

Amelia was waiting for us with Anita Johnson, who by now knew the whole story. If the commander recognised me she never said.

I had desperately been trying to think of a way to get rid of Mac, and oddly enough it was Amelia who came up with the solution which was so obvious I hadn't thought of it.

"I think that horrible man should be arrested.

Kidnapping is a very serious offence. He shouldn't be allowed to get away with it." She fussed about seating the children and finding them some fruit juice.

"Stay here." I told them, "At least then I'll know you're safe. I'll be back shortly." Then to Amelia, "If I have a problem I will call you," and I was away.

On my way down the stairs I dialled the police and reported the kidnapping of John and Carli. I gave my name and told them what I knew. I'd arranged to meet them at the Sixth Airport Hotel so flagged down a cab and was on my way. Sixth was the furthest hotel from the Airport but it took only fifteen minutes to get there. Reception refused to give out MacKenzie's room number, so I waited for the squad vehicle.

"This is my son he's holding and a very vulnerable 18 year old girl. I know they are technically of age, but they have been missing for four days and brought here against their will. That is kidnapping and illegal."

The two officers burst into the room, fire arms at the ready, and assessed the scene before them. Two teenagers, a girl and a boy both wrapped in towels, with their hands and feet bound with plastic ties. Mac stormed out of the bathroom.

"Professor Harrison MacKenzie? You are under arrest on the charge of kidnapping Miss Carli Meredith Cavendish and Mr John Rawlings." They proceeded to read him his rights and handcuff him. Then, after assuring John that his father would be here shortly, they marched him to the elevator and thence, I assumed, into their transport.

"They could've cut these ties," John moaned, grumpily, "they're too tight."

"I can do that," I said entering the room. "Looks

like I need to find you some clothes, too," seeing theirs draped over chairs to dry.

I hugged them both. We'd never been so relieved to see each other.

"Now, clothes."

"Don't worry, we can wear these, they're almost dry," they both lied together. They were so anxious to get away while they could. I wasn't going to argue.

While they dressed I rang James. "I've got them. They're safe and well. Call soon. Over and out."

We were about to leave when Carli cried out, "E-Tec!" and dashed into the main bedroom. "Andrew," she yelled, "come and help!" Eventually they emerged clutching phones, watches passports and her precious e-Tec.

39

The meeting

Wednesday August 29th 2265

Evening

At the First Airport Hotel, Otto brought us all the way to the eighteenth floor. Apparently this was his suite, which he shared with Jay and Andrew. It's very similar to the one we'd left, but a lot nicer and definitely larger. Two bathrooms, which is good, and lots of dry towels. I grinned, remembering Mac's reaction when he discovered Andrew had accidentally dropped the last dry one into the water. Maybe that was why he tied our feet and wrists? Out of spite? At least the cops knew we were telling the truth.

"If you go through to Jay's room you'll find clothes your size, so you can get out of those soggy ones you're wearing. Same, John, applies to you." He pointed towards the other room. Roll your wet things in the towels, it will help them to dry. "We'll be a bit squashed in here, but it's only for one night, so we'll have to manage."

I must admit it was nice to put on clean, dry clothing. Everything fitted, but then I shouldn't be surprised, we are, after all identical. I hoped my clone wouldn't mind my borrowing them. I chose the top I liked the least, thinking that she wouldn't mind as much. A thought suddenly struck me as I went back to the main living room.

"Otto, if these are Jay and Andrew's things does this mean we shall be meeting them?"

"It does. At the moment they are with a friend in another suite downstairs. I don't want you all to meet for the first time with others present. What I will do is bring them here so you can have some privacy to get to know each other."

How did I feel about that? I don't know. He dialled a number on the hotel phone and spoke quietly to someone.

"I have some important things to arrange and will be back in about forty minutes."

I began to feel nervous. A short while later there was a knock on the door. In walked Andrew and me!

I got such a shock. I mean I was expecting them but they were so real! Does that sound silly, they are our doubles after all. The only way to differentiate between us would be by our names, so I must remember to call Andrew John and think of myself as Carli.

For a long minute we stared at each other, not knowing what to say or do. Then Jay came forward and gave me a hug.

"I gather you've had a pretty rough time, being kidnapped and all," she said. The two Andrew's just stood with their mouths open, like bewildered goldfish. I drew Jay's attention to them and we burst out laughing. From then on I knew it would be OK.

"I hope it's all right but I've borrowed some of your clothes. We were captive for four days and as soon

229

as Mac took us to the other hotel I bagged the bathroom and washed me and most of my filthy clothes. They were still very wet when we arrived here. Otto thought you wouldn't mind."

Jay laughed and offered to dry my hair. "Of course not! You might have chosen a nicer top though, I've never really liked that one but hadn't the heart to tell Otto. This feels so odd. It's like finding I have a sister, who I've never met. Do you know, I think it's rather nice. I've never had a sister before. Fate has thrown us together."

The boys, meanwhile had joined in our laughter but by now were discussing maths problems. I caught the tail end of a bit about somebody or other's theorem. Jay had heard them too, we rolled eyes saying together,"Boys!"

"No," I said. "Andrew's!" and we danced around hugging each other in fits of giggles.

It was so nice to have company my own age. Well, I know I've always had John but it's not the same as having a sister. We retreated to the bathroom and found the hair-drier, although by now it was almost dry. It felt so good to be clean.

"I know it's a daft question, but have you met my, your, no, our father?"

I sensed Jay had been wanting to ask this since she first arrived. "It's not a silly question at all. John and I are staying with them. By them I mean Papa, his lovely wife Elise and their gorgeous, boisterous four year old twins, Fabian and Xavier. And we see a lot of Elise's parents, Henri and Françoise. In case you haven't guessed they have a very French heritage and all live in Paris."

230

"Wow! A whole ready made family." Jay had a sadness in her eye. It wasn't envy or regret, although maybe it was, that she could never be part of it. I must not dwell on this, I thought.

"Where were you when we arrived here?" I asked.

"On the third floor with two very nice ladies, mother and daughter."

No, surely not, she'd told Mac they were flying to London this evening, but still it was worth asking.

"Did the younger woman have an Australian accent and the older lady was very British with white hair and mischievous eyes?"

"Yes, I asked Anita about her accent and she said she lived in Queensland. I didn't like to ask where that was, but Andrew knew. He seems to know everything."

"What an amazing coincidence that they should be here. At this hotel. I think it was because of her that Otto found us and rescued us. I gave her a note to phone Papa, when we met in the airport Ladies room. You know the police marched into our hotel room brandishing their guns and arrested Mac. I hope they lock him up forever and ever." I suddenly realised how childish this had sounded, but somehow I knew Jay understood.

"Are you in love with John?"

I looked at her and, yes, Jay was serious. "Don't know, haven't even thought about it. I do know that I'd be happy to spend the rest of my life with him. Couldn't imagine being without him now."

"I was sure I was in love with Wesley once. Did you know the others? Yes, of course you did. You were there instead of us. Did you like Catalina? We were besties. There's a film of her playing her 'Colour Music' she called it. Her piano was in the great observation lounge and we all used to listen to it. Delman's scathing remarks were ignored and eventually he gave up. He was really nasty sometimes."

I thought back to my colour music and to everything that happened before. And suddenly I was there, back on the Temeraire, listening to Catalina playing her music, my music, but it wasn't mine any more. I am glad that she enjoys her new gift and I only miss it occasionally. I must ask Jay about their friendship. Should I tell her she's her half sister?

Once again it was John who brought me back to reality. Not with a nudge but by knocking on the door. "You girls going to be in there all night?"

We joined 'The Andrews' as they had become to us as Otto returned.

"I see you haven't murdered each other," he said, jokingly. "If you are ready we will go down to the dining room?"

"Yes!" I said, the boys getting up to go.

"No!" This was Jay. "Not in that tee-shirt, come with me." I followed her through to her bedroom and she handed me a lovely green and orange top, very like the first one I'd worn on the Endeavour. Then she pinned my hair back with a gold clasp.

"Ready," we announced.

"The ladies will be joining us, I hope that is in order". Otto had gone back to his awkwardness again, but I didn't mind, it suited him.

I was delighted to see my old lady again and Commander Johnson. What a truly amazing coincidence.

She told me about her phone call with Papa. I

looked anxiously at Otto, who nodded and mouthed he knows you're safe.

"Can I ask you something?" I said to Amelia.

Eyes twinkling, she smiled.

"When you were in conversation with Mac you said you were flying to London this evening, why?"

"Well, if you had listened carefully you'd have heard me say that we fly at eight. So we do, eight in the morning. I just wanted to confuse the issue, put him off the scent."

Everyone was listening to us.

"I can do a very good impersonation of a dotty old lady when necessary. It comes in useful. I found out all I needed to know from your arrogant professor. Like so many highly intelligent people he has very little common sense! He never even realised, he was so full of his own self importance."

"You were wonderful. I don't know how we can ever thank you." Then I had an idea. "I don't suppose you are going to be in Paris on Friday?"

"May one ask why?"

"It's just that…..." I hesitated, would Otto approve? I didn't even know if it would be possible to get extra tickets. Was I being crazy? I picked up 'great idea' from John. Remembering to call him John had become easier now there were the four of us.

"She does this sometimes," he said, "no, quite a lot really. Goes off into her own little world. It must be something writers do. Jay! No!," he shook his head, "Carli, come back to us."

"I'm not surprised you got the name wrong. They are so alike. Now what were you going to say about Paris on Friday?" She was astute, Amelia, and I had a feeling she suspected something unusual was going on.

"I don't even know if we can get tickets, but I would truly love you both to be there if possible."

"Where, dear? I know it's Paris but what's the occasion?"

"It's a live television show, in the evening." There I'd said it. Otto didn't seem to mind. I so much wanted these lovely ladies to be there and know the truth, before it hit the general media. I wanted them to meet Papa and Elise and almost be part of the family.

"Are you going to give me any more clues? The usual expression is trying to get blood out of a stone, but this more akin to moving Stonehenge half a metre to the left!" Amelia was laughing as she said this and so was everyone else.

"What John's very clever girl friend is trying to tell you is that she has written an amazing book which is to be launched and reviewed on 'Is This Rubbish' Friday evening." Otto took out his Satfone, "If you will excuse me, I shall call James now and ask him about extra tickets."

He was gone for a long time, well, I suppose it was only ten minutes but it seemed like forever as I daren't say anything about the book, what it was about about or even called. John and Andrew came to my rescue and changed the subject but it didn't do much for my embarrassment. I felt really mean.

"Sorry to be so long. I needed to call the police, having missed a call while we were eating. It's rather odd, they are transferring Mac to a holding zone up state for some reason they are not specifying. Tickets, not a problem. If you are able to come that is?"

"That's good, I hoped he could swing it." Amelia

looked like a cat who'd got the cream.

"Mother! What have you done?"

"Nothing really, I only thought that these lovely young people had been through enough with that nasty professor, and I didn't want him to be released and come after them again. So I rang George and asked him to make things more difficult for him if he could."

Anita was laughing as she explained. George was Chief of the Airport Police and happens to be her sister's husband.

I really did find the right person to give my note to, I thought.

Otto continued, "We do, though, have a problem with flights. There are two seats available on our Paris flight but Jay and Andrew can't use them."

"Why?" I don't know how many said this but we all wanted to know.

"Because you can't travel on identical passports. Jay and Andrew travelled on replicas of Carli and John's passports- it's a long story. I was hoping to get two of you on a different airline. If the planes left at the same time we should get away with it. Now we have a problem."

"Carli and John can use our tickets. It's more important for them to get back for the show than us. We can follow later." Jay looked hopeful.

Amelia was thoughtful, "There's always our booking to London."

"Mother, what are you thinking?"

"Well, Paris is a mere hop from London. You can even use the train if you have to. If we nab the Paris seats and cancel ours for London then they'll be available for Jay and Andrew. You know it's a good idea. Come along, Anita, do some phoning."

Anita knew better than to argue with her mother. Soon it was all settled. We would fly to Paris with Anita and Amelia, and Andrew, Jay and Otto to London. Both flights were due to leave at 8am so all we needed to do was pray that we wouldn't get stopped.

In the lift Jay and I thanked Otto for a lovely meal and she said how much she agreed with him about eating and conversation being one of the finer things of life. A sudden thought; is this why we have to sit and chat for half an hour at pill time? A hangover from Earth?

40

A fright at the airport

Thursday August 30th 2265

It's nice to have my e-Tec back, I was so lost without it. Last night I managed to transfer everything from the last few days. I know we were supposed to be going to sleep because of the early start today, but both Jay and I wanted to get things down while they were fresh in our minds. It was so funny. We sat on the bed with our backs to each other dictating the events. I started first, while Jay was in the shower. By the time she picked up her e-Tec we were both saying the same things. Like an echo. It's uncanny how alike we are.

We needed to be at the Airport for six. We checked in for our flights and then all had breakfast together. Most enjoyable. Amelia surprised me by taking charge and organising everyone. She is a delightful person, I'm so glad she will be at the show. She insisted that Otto take Jay and Andrew through the customs check before she went through with us.

Then it was our turn. I must admit that I was feeling nervous. Customs people have a way of scrutinising you which makes me feel guilty. The fact that we were travelling on duplicate passports made it worse. Then the customs man said, "Mrs Barrington-Smythe, will you and your party come with me please?"

My heart sank. This was it. Bang goes the show, I thought. No sense in panicking, Papa would manage. Maybe Jay could impersonate me? But did she know enough to carry it off? Oh, heck.

We were taken to a small side room. Amelia took everything in her stride and calmly sat down. Anita looked flustered and John paced up and down. Finally this cop arrived and I thought we were all going to be arrested.

"Hello Ma in Law, Anita. I'm sorry to keep you waiting. Curiosity got the better of me and I couldn't resist meeting your two young heroes."

I was so relieved. We were introduced to George. Anita explained that he was her twin sister's husband. I thought it a shame that they lived so far from each other, one in Australia the other in America and their mum, I assumed, in England.

John picked this up. "Not as far away as Mars," he said out loud. Then realised what he's done. Really he does have balmy moments sometimes. I wondered if Andrew was the same. Jay had told me they'd played chess together on the Discovery. Now there's a thought, what would happen if we set the boys up to play each other? Amelia was looking at him, an interesting expression on her face that I couldn't read. I think she's suspicious about something but doesn't know what. That sounds so crazy…..

A sharp nudge from John brought me back to what was going on. "Daydreaming as usual. George has just asked you about your book."

Amelia stepped in. "You won't get any information on that front, it's all very hush, hush. Anita and I will be at the launch tomorrow and it's a no go zone until then."

"Well, I wish you good luck with it. You must come back to New York when you're rich and famous. Maybe write about our exciting city."

"I have every intention of doing exactly that. We've fallen in love with the 'Big Apple'."

"Now, dears, our flight will be boarding soon so we need to be on our way. Goodbye, George. Give Charlotte and the children a hug for me. Come along everyone." Amelia ushered us through to the correct waiting area.

Later

Papa met us with Henri and Françoise. It was decided that Amelia and Anita would stay with them, while Jay and Andrew would share with us when they arrived. Apparently Otto's sleeps very well on the playroom sofa. They aren't due in Paris until later this afternoon. Poor things they will be exhausted.

41

Amelia to the rescue

Friday August 31st 2265

D-Day is finally here. Having planned this for two months I can't believe it's really going to happen. I wish Otto and the others were back. He rang through last night to say there had been a problem with their Paris flight. They'd tried other airports but nothing until Saturday, which was too late. They have seats booked on the Paris Express which arrives at five thirty this afternoon. Cutting it fine as they still had to get to the studio and we were supposed to be there for briefing at six. Why does nothing ever go smoothly? No, that's unfair, I had only to think back to how we were rescued and our own flight here to disprove it.

So now I must get up and think about what to wear tonight. I hope Elise will help with that.

I wasn't the only one thinking about this, it was the big discussion point at breakfast, and afterwards when Amelia and everyone else arrived.

"You have to decide on the impact you want to make, dear." Amelia had put a lot of thought into this, I could tell. "Do you want to emphasize your individuality or the fact that you are absolutely identical."

Everyone started talking at once, except John, who

stared at me with an expression I didn't understand. Then I did. He was thinking about weddings, of all things. What was he on? Indignantly I thought, well, ask me then don't mess about.

"What about it?" He asked out loud, with a silly grin.

Oh, no, you're not going to get away with that, I thought.

"About what?" was my mischievous answer. I must admit that since Jay had asked me if I was in love with John I had been thinking about him in a very different way. But I wasn't going to play this game.

"You know," he said sheepishly.

Acting the innocent, "I have no idea what you're talking about." I'd make him squirm.

I should say here that conversation had ceased and all eyes were upon us. I'm sure he hadn't noticed. What he did then I shall never ever forget. It was unbelievably embarrassing. I guess it served me right. He got up and stood directly in front of me. Then he sat on the carpet and, in his adorable, blunt, Andrew sort of way, said, "I think it would be a good idea if we got married. We can't stay here forever and we can't live together otherwise and I'm certainly not wanting to live on my own. You can't cook so you can't be on your own either. Oh crumbs, I've made a right idiot of myself." He raised himself so he was balancing on one knee, wobbling a bit. "I adore you, Carli. Will you marry me?"

Thank heavens for telepathy, I thought, otherwise it would have been a total shock. I wondered if the Andrews had been talking about us.

"Well, say something." They were all waiting for

me.

"I don't know, I'll have to think about it." I tried to hold my expression of complete innocence. His face was a picture, I thought he was going to cry. Then he caught my smile and we burst into laughter.

"Of course I will. But do get up off the floor you twit....... Ah! Put me down!" This whirling around trick of his is getting to be a habit.

There followed joyous scenes of happy congratulations and kissing. "Papa, I hope he asked you first."

"Was I meant to, oh crumbs, it never occurred to me. Oh! Um, er, James, can I marry your beautiful, amazing, gorgeous, wonderful, clever, talented daughter?"

"Providing your prospects are good enough to keep her in the manner to which she has been accustomed." A typical, light hearted, Papa type response.

"Well, I can certainly do better than anything they've got on Mars......." He paused, closed his eyes and then said, "Uh oh, shouldn't have got so carried away."

"Actually Anita guessed and told me, dears. Is that what your book is about, life on Mars? No, it's unfair of me to ask, we shall be content to wait until tonight."

Finally it was decided what we should wear. This involved a quick visit to the local boutique. Well, it was supposed to be quick but with five women in one shop and three men and the twins in another, all with differing ideas it took all morning. We had a late lunch out and I wondered how Jay and Andrew were doing. Time was getting on. By five o'clock there was still no

242

word not even when we had to leave for the studio. I was rapidly becoming a nervous wreck.

The Show

Six pm and here we are. The producer welcomed us and enthused about my diary. It *had* been chosen for their 'Book of the Month,' I couldn't believe it. He went on and on about how vivid my imagination was. I have no imagination, I thought, you wait till the interview. I wondered if he'd be annoyed that we'd deceived him and used his show to get publicity, but then if this was the sort of show Papa had told us it was, surely he would be pleased if we created a stir.

I was wearing a very simple scarlet strappy dress, which was knee length and had a lovely drape to it. Red shoes with a low heel. I didn't feel steady in higher ones and if I didn't I was certain that Jay wouldn't. My hair was brushed back and taken to the side with a lovely sparkly green and gold clasp. I'd wanted red but the shop only had the one and we needed two. The idea was for us to look identical.

The show started at seven and all the other stuff came first. We had been warned that we'd be called on stage about twenty past. The others still haven't arrived, what's keeping them? We'll have to manage without them.

"Don't be frightened, hold your own. You may get some bad reaction from the audience, there's always some opposition, but don't let it get to you. What you must remember is not to alienate them." This was James advice. He would be introducing us. It never occurred to me to ask why.

243

The voice of the show's host suddenly became clearer. "Now, Ladies and Gentlemen time for our Book of the Month, which, in view of the current renewed interest in good old fashioned books, is available in hard copy and on sale at several points in the auditorium. Before I invite someone you are all familiar with to introduce our new author, we have time for a word from our sponsors."

By this time I was all of a fluster! There was a scuffle behind us as Jay and Andrew arrived with Otto. Thank goodness. I ran over and hugged her, got told off by the director so returned to wait with John. Wardrobe had been given their instructions by an insistent Amelia, so I knew she would be OK.

"Welcome back to our Book of the Month. This has been written by a new, very young writer, such talent and imagination is unusual for an eighteen year old. Here to introduce her is her father James Cavendish, better known to you all as Charlie Fenn."

Charlie Fenn, I thought, who's Charlie Fenn? I wasn't concentrating, luckily the producer was and he pushed us on stage at the appropriate moment, to deafening applause. I hadn't expected that. I looked at John, this is it, I thought. Oh heck, I can't do this. Then I spotted Amelia sitting in the middle of the front row. She smiled, nodding encouragingly.

Everything I'd thought of saying had gone from my mind. My stomach was churning over and I felt sick. Papa was saying something and as one the audience went, "Aah!" He'd only gone and introduced John as my fiancée adding that it was today we had become engaged. I was well and truly flummoxed.

"Miss Cavendish, or may I call you Carli, what

prompted you to write your book? What was your inspiration?"

I swallowed and said in a small voice, "It is important to tell the world what is happening on Mars. The public need to know how the Guardians with their perfectionist opinions treat those who live there."

"Come now, Carli. This story of yours is just that, a story, an imaginary diary written by a dreamy eighteen year old girl."

For goodness sake don't patronise her, she'll flip! I caught this from John and it was as well that I had, because he was right. He came to my rescue, as he had so often before.

He stood, addressing the audience and, as usual, went straight to the point. "How many of you are over the age of eighty?" A few reluctant hands went up, including Amelia's. I gave her a quizzing look and she winked at me. I love you, I thought.

"How many of you have elderly parents, relatives, friends who are over the age of eighty?" Now almost every hand was gradually raised, and there was an interested hush.

"If you live on Mars your life is terminated at the age of eighty, and no one knows the Guardians are doing it. That is why Carli has published the diary that she wrote while we were both on board a Termination Vessel, the USS Temeraire."

He paused. People were quiet. I'd have thought this would have created a stir but it was a stunned silence. Then I remembered how I felt when we first discovered the truth.

John hadn't finished. "Ladies and Gentleman, one more thing. In the front row I can see several wheelchairs. Disability is something not allowed on Mars because it is classed as imperfection within the Guardian's utopian city of Newton-Aldrin. As soon as a child is born with a problem he or she is cloned. Then, when the time is right, which as far as I can work out is when schooling is over at approximately eighteen years, they are taken for a three month trip on the Temeraire, from which they never return."

He paused again to let them think about this.

"These disadvantaged children are cloned and their clones are returned to Mars assuming the identity of the original child."

"If you read the book you will learn how this is achieved." He was an amazing instinctive public speaker, talking slowly, allowing time for each important phrase to sink in.

"Life on Mars is very different from Earth. Everything is censored. Jay and I knew nothing of World Wars or violence of any kind until we travelled to Earth. A Martian eighteen year old has the same street age as a twelve or thirteen year old here on Earth."

He sat down.

"What happens to them?" someone shouted.

"Their bodies are disposed of. Vaporised," was John's reply.

Then there was uproar. People stood up and shouted.

"And now a word from our sponsors!"

"What the hell are you two playing at?" The show's host was furious.

"Papa said you liked a nice bit of controversy" I'd put on my innocent, butter wouldn't melt look I'd

246

learned from the twins. I wondered who was looking after them as I could see Elise, Henri, Françoise and Anita all in the front row with Amelia. She caught my eye. I knew there was something not quite right, she was saying, now I understand. But not out loud. Did I have a telepathy with her, too?

The producer had come over and said something to our host who looked even more explosive. But I saw him swallow and take a deep breath.

"Welcome back to our Book of the Month. It seems we have an interesting scenario, Ladies and Gentlemen, Miss Carli Cavendish is claiming that her story is not a figure of her imagination after all." He almost spat my name.

There was a noise behind me as someone came on stage. My turn now. I ignored the idiot host and stood up, turning to face what I hoped were Jay and Andrew. I was wrong. It was two people I've never seen before wearing Mars uniform. Oh, what a brilliant idea, I thought.

"Now it's my turn," I said hoping they would quieten down and listen. I spoke almost in a whisper to get their attention. "We are now going to have a fashion show. Ladies, this is what you wear on Mars, all day, everyday, from the day you are born until the day you are terminated."

Both figures came forward and walked across the stage, turning and showing off the hideous, shapeless garments as models on a catwalk. Thank you, I thought, absolutely perfect.

"No jeans, no dresses, no individuality. Nothing wears out. Babies and children wear the same garments in different sizes as they grow. The Guardians say it is

247

because of transportation costs. But ladies, imagine not owning your own clothes? Not even being able to choose or wear a wedding dress."

I let that sink in whilst I delved into my bag and found some headache pills. They weren't the right ones but would do to illustrate the point.

"On Mars we do not have the pleasure of eating meals together. How long does it take to swallow a pill three times a day? The Guardians say that transportation costs prohibit the eating of proper food. No lovely long lunches with your family and friends. No going to a restaurant for a Birthday or special occasion. No glass of wine or Champagne. Not even a cup of coffee, only water, always water. Pills three times a day and a large glass of recycled water."

I listened to the silence.

I couldn't think of anything else to say, so looked at John who was grinning, obviously delighted with the way things were going. Papa looked pleased. The host was scowling.

There was a general murmuring and then someone stood and said, "What about the clones. There's no such thing!"

Oops, I'd almost forgotten Jay and Andrew. I stood up again.

"We have been cloned, John and I. We would never have been able to leave Mars without help." Quiet once again. "Allow me to introduce Jay and Andrew."

Otto, stood at the side, was gently pushing them on stage with a massive grin on his face. Awkwardly they came forward greeted by gasps from the audience, which changed into increasingly louder murmuring. I

248

was thankful they had read the diary and therefore weren't completely in the dark. Jay looked gorgeous in her red dress and I was so glad about the shoes. They weren't flat, but the heel was sturdy and there was a pretty bow on the front. Her hair had been brushed till it shone and pinned back exactly as mine. I went forward and hugged them both. "It's OK I whispered, just be yourselves."

"All right for you," moaned Andrew. He was not prepared for being the centre of attention.

I don't know what reaction I expected from our audience, but not the one we received.

"This is rubbish!"

"They're twins!"

"It's all a sham!"

These were comments I heard, there were lots I didn't. There was general booing and hissing. All I kept hearing in my head were Papa's words, "Don't alienate your audience." Oh heck, John transmitted, what do we do now? Should we prepare to make a dash for the exit? The crowd were more like an aggressive angry mob and, quite frankly terrifying. I was frightened and looked to the host for help. But he was smug, smirking, keeping silent. I couldn't believe it.

Unexpected help did arrive. During all the noise and chaos Amelia, coolly and calmly made her way onto the stage. She stood in the centre and waited patiently, until once more there was order.

"Ladies and gentlemen," she began in her beautiful precise English. "I am the mother of identical twins. My daughters were so alike that they were forced to wear name tags all the time at school. I was the only person who could differentiate between them, even their father couldn't and they had some fun with him because of this, I can tell you."

This brought a titter of laughter. She has them eating out of her hand, I thought. Amelia, how do you do it?

"When I first saw these young people together yesterday, I realised they were not twins. They are too alike. I knew my girls apart because they had their own personality's, their own expressions and their own way of thinking. And in this respect they were very different. I think with most sets of twins one is dominant and the other a follower. There is one mark of identification. The only visual difference for my girls is a birth mark on Charlotte's right thigh. Anita does not have this.

She came over and stood between Jay and me. Taking us each by the hand she led us to the front of the stage. I wondered what was coming.

"This morning, while choosing outfits for this show I noticed something very unusual."

She turned towards the cameraman on her right, saying, "Young man, I want you to zoom in and concentrate on these young ladies." He obeyed and I noticed a twinkle in his eye

"Now, dear," she said to me, "turn round." She held me with my back to the camera.

"Ladies and gentlemen, do you see a birth mark, here towards her left shoulder blade?" This was news to me. I'd never known about it before, but then I wouldn't. Wearing Mars uniform, it would always have been covered, and I'd never bothered much with mirrors, what was the point?

"It is the shape of an apple, a closer shot will

reveal even the stalk." She beckoned to the cameraman, pointed to the spot and waited for the image to appear on a massive screen in the studio.

"Jay, will you turn round please." There by her shoulder blade in exactly the same position, according to Amelia, was an identical birth mark.

"This could never naturally occur. One of these young ladies is a clone of the other and even I am not certain which is which. Now, I have no personal knowledge of young John's body. James, you were with him earlier while clothes shopping. Did you notice anything of significance?"

Poor Papa looked very nonplussed, but before he could answer Otto appeared. Amelia took her cue. "Ladies and Gentlemen, this is John's father." She still held her audience.

Otto came forward, to the front of the stage, ignoring the host man who tried to intervene. He grabbed hold of one of the Andrew's on his way and brought him too.

"Good evening, Ladies and Gentlemen." He beamed at the audience and they welcomed him with applause. "John does have a distinguishing mark, luckily not in an embarrassing place." Again the audience response was good, with a ripple of laughter.

"There are three little moles which form a perfect equilateral triangle."

Thanks Otto, I thought, how many of this mob would even know what that is?

"They are positioned to the right of his naval."

I waited, amused to see what would happen, catching John's sense of fun too. Duly revealed, there was the triangle of moles. Before the crowd turned again John stepped forward.

"Actually, Dad, you've got the wrong one, I'm John." Laughing he revealed his own identical trio of moles by his belly button. It was captured by the zoom lens and projected onto the screen, to the delight and uproar of the audience.

Our host took control. "And now, over to our sponsors."

That was a long gap, I thought, maybe he was told not to interrupt Amelia. I don't think he'd have dared anyway.

After the ads it was almost the end of the show. The host tried to reassert his authority, but the producer appeared on stage carrying an ink-pad and paper which he placed on the coffee table. He raised his hands for quiet. "Ladies and Gentlemen, as the producer of 'Is This Rubbish?' I have a request for John and Andrew."

They stepped forward, grinning, knowing exactly what he was on about, while Jay and I were clueless.

"Thumb or forefinger?" asked Andrew. The camera zoomed in on the ink-pad and paper as Andrew pressed his right index finger into the pad, rolling it from side to side as he's seen in the movies. Carefully he made a print on the paper.

It was now John's turn and he played out the drama beautifully. He held up his right index finger to the audience and to the camera, then picked up the paper with Andrew's mark, displaying it like a magician around the width of the studio. He smiled at Amelia and asked her to take Andrew to the far side of the stage, before he sat beside the coffee table to make his print next to the other. He rolled up his sleeve, taking his time, milking the occasion. Even I was willing him to get on with it. Our amused cameraman closed in, capturing his every move, a mesmerised audience concentrated on the big screen while he made his mark. John clicked his fingers at our miserable host for a pen and initialled his print before holding the paper up for the cameraman who must have been ready with a special magnifying lens, which slowly superimposed one print over the other.

As one the audience gasped, followed by silence and then a thunderous applause. The prints were identical, every line, every tiny smudge. The zoom lens covered every detail of them.

The interviewer tried to wind things up but was drowned out and I saw the producers arm slice sideways, presumably signifying the end of the show.

I tuned out and started thinking about John. It would be nice when we were on our own again and could go back to being ourselves once more. Was he serious about getting married, surely not. He came over and kissed me, on the lips, before I could stop him. You rat! I thought and then I realised that I'd rather enjoyed it, so kissed him back. It was only afterwards that I had doubts about him being my Andrew, John. His eyes were laughing at me, and I knew he was the right one.

The auditorium was clearing, it was over. Now all we had to do was wait for the fallout.

42

The real McCoy

Friday August 31st 2265

Afterwards

The producer was with Papa for a while after the show, but I don't know whether he thought it had gone well or not. Jay and I chatted with the Andrews until everyone else arrived.

"How did you know about the birth mark?" I asked Amelia. "Not mine, I mean Jay's."

"A little secret, I didn't and I really held my breath as she turned round. But there it was. You see I had absolute faith in you and John. I also know a lot about twins."

"Well you were wonderful. I was really scared when things turned nasty. I was picking up from John that he wanted to do a runner and for me to get ready to dash out." Oops, I'd said too much, again. Neither of us is very good at keeping secrets, I thought. Luckily everyone was talking at the same time and Amelia and I were on our own.

"So there is a telepathy between the two of you?" Was this a question or a statement? I wasn't sure. There was something about this woman that was so special, we were definitely on the same wavelength. She seemed to reach inside my soul.

She took my non answer to be a yes and as Anita approached she touched the side of her nose with her index finger, as she had before. I must ask her what it means.

The Producer was very happy with the programme. People had been phoning all the time to ask about the book. The show had ended up with almost double their normal audience ratings. He congratulated John and I on the way we had introduced our subject matter and handled a difficult situation. He didn't seem to mind that he had almost been tricked into making it 'Book of the Month.' Then he turned to Amelia.

"Dear Lady. Thank you for saving the whole evening. It needed a miracle to turn that audience round and you did it. A very delicate situation, which took a great deal of courage. You must be used to speaking in public."

"No," she said with a smile, "but I knew I was right. I also know a great deal about twins."

People were clearing stuff around us. My two 'Martians' were talking to Elise and Papa, so I excused myself and went to thank them. They had done their job perfectly.

"I understand congratulations are in order." Otto stood behind me, looking pleased.

I wondered what he meant, then caught on. "I'm not sure he was serious, it was so chaotic this morning."

"Ah."

Otto has a way of saying that two letter word, pronouncing it like no one else. "I think you'll find he is."

Nonchalantly I replied, "We'll see."

We were all hungry. We'd only had a cup of tea and some cake before leaving home.

"A celebratory meal," Papa announced. "Umberto is expecting us, so people, let's go!" He lead the way out of the building and along the road.

Cheerfully we formed a crocodile to one of his favourite restaurants. John was delighted to be eating an Italian meal again. "Do I dare ask for Zabaglione? Last time I did the chef in Romano's threw a tantrum."

Trust him to be thinking of puddings. He held me close as we walked along behind the rest. "Are you serious?" I asked.

"About?"

"Us getting married?"

"Of course. Oh darn I forgot to tell Andrew I'd done it!"

"Andrew? What's Andrew got to do with it?" So they had talked about us, well me anyway.

"He bet me a bar of chocolate that I wouldn't have the guts to ask you before the show!"

I stood still, turned to face him, fuming. Just as I was about to let rip he giggled. "You are so gorgeous when you're angry. You react so well."

"John!" I yelled as he charged down the street after the others.

The meal was delicious. We ordered lots of different items so Jay and Andrew could try things as we'd done before on the Endeavour. Umberto himself was there and he'd been delighted to see us. When John tried his luck for Zabaglione, Umberto disappeared into the kitchen. He returned with a trolley complete with wide copper pan and a large container of boiling water over a spirit stove and all the ingredients for this delicate dessert, thus making John his coveted Italian pudding in front of us. Now I understood why the busy chef in Romano's threw a wobbly. This is a dish, which has to made individually for each order, required his complete attention for nearly ten minutes.

"I must learn to make that. It was wonderful." John had had a long discussion with Umberto, so I presumed he was asking about the recipe. There had been enough mixture to give Jay and Andrew some and they were definitely hooked.

"Papa, who is Charlie Fenn?"

"Me," he said, or rather my nom de plume. I write historical detective stories and they have quite a following. That's how I knew the producer. Though I doubt he'll have me back again."

"Oh Papa, I'm sorry. I've been so wrapped up in my own silly diary it never occurred to me that I might have spoiled things for you, have I?"

"Good heavens no! You've done the programme a huge favour. Our host, Quentin, was not a happy bunny, but the producer was overjoyed."

I decided not to ask what rabbits had to with the obnoxious Quentin. I was getting used to Papa's little colloquialisms, it would wait.

"I forgot to tell you that they sold all the copies they had, that's eight hundred books. They've never done that before. They wanted you to sign them but I said you were far too exhausted and needed to go home and get some rest."

We were interrupted by Umberto bearing a silver tray with Champagne and glasses followed by what looked like his entire staff coming from the kitchen.

He stopped before John and me, "Congratulations," he announced his face beaming with pleasure. "We all wish you every happiness."

John's cue, he stood behind his chair. "Thank you Umberto and your team for your kind wishes and for the most delicious meal. I am determined to learn how to make Zabaglione. Thank you to Jay and Andrew for coming all this way to support us, under difficult conditions. Thank you Amelia for so much this evening and for passing clandestine messages, and helping things along. Thank you Elise for all your cooking lessons and your fabulous meals. Thank you Henri, Françoise and Anita for your friendship and support. Thank you Dad for rescuing us. Thank you James for letting me marry Carli."

What a nice idea to say thank you, well done, I thought, but he hadn't finished.

"Oh um, ta for saying yes Phillie!" and he ducked behind his chair much to everyone's amusement.

THE END

Epilogue

The story really ended with the show and John's thank you speech, but there are a few loose ends that need tying up.

Fallout, as I'd called it was an accurate name for what happened next day and for several days, come to that. It started with the house phone ringing at some awful hour in the morning. It never rang again so I guess it was left disconnected. When I peered round the curtain to check the weather there was a crowd of people waiting outside in the street. I wished it would rain really hard and wash them away. How the press got to know where we were is beyond me. At least I'd assumed they were press and Elise confirmed this when she arrived with welcome mugs of tea for us.

"We must do our best to ignore them until we've had a family conference and decided what to say." She reassured me. "Papa and James will know what to do."

"I'm sorry, Elise, I thought last night was the difficult bit, I'm not so sure now. Will the boys be frightened by all the attention?"

"They've discovered Uncle Otto on their sofa and are very happy playing with him. They are delighted that you and John are twins like themselves. Come down when you're ready, no hurry."

In the kitchen the boys were eating breakfast with Papa, Otto and the Andrews.

"More twins!" the little ones yelled, clapping and cheering. "Twins are best!" Making high fives with the

Andrew's.

Not long after there was a stir outside, Henri and the others had arrived.

"That was a fight!" he declared. We progressed to the sitting room with some fresh coffee, for the discussion. Papa had drawn the curtains to keep out prying eyes.

"I think we need to begin with some good news." Papa surprised us all, particularly me as I couldn't think of anything good about all this.

"My, no, *your* publisher, Carli, rang my personal phone. The book has gone into reprint of five hundred thousand. An amazing achievement when you consider that most people will read it electronically. And they are prepared to have further reprints if necessary."

I picked up John's 'I told you so' thoughts, but ignored them, even if I did sort of agree. I'm not sure how I feel about this news. It's good that lots of people would find out about the awful happenings on Mars, but what about us, here, now? Had we dumped Otto and Papa in real trouble by exposing that they revealed to us the Guardian's plans? The secret V machine? Would we all face trial? Would they be exiled as well as us? At least Mac is in custody already, well, hopefully they hadn't let him go yet. But we weren't even sure of that.

"John to Carli! Wakey, wakey! You're the only one whose not pleased about your book."

"Oh I am, yes of course I am. I'm so worried about Otto and Papa. I don't want them to go to jail because of this. You know, with the vaporiser being top secret."

Amelia who'd been quietly listening came to life. "Both British are you?" She demanded of Otto.

"We needed official citizenship when we were at

Oxford. Mac too, for what it's worth," he confirmed.

"Reggie! He'll sort you out."

Before anyone could enquire as to who Reggie was, Amelia enlightened us. "My husband, Reginald Barrington-Smythe. Leading Barrister with a definite anti-establishment bias. Always up for a challenge. He'll delight in this case. Opt to be tried under British Law and I'd lay money on it no jury will convict you. There has been so much disquiet, unrest, even riots about recent laws and restrictions made by the Guardians. The country is rebelling. Something we British do extremely well. There is a huge movement against their policies in the UK."

She paused a moment, smiling. "Persuade MacKenzie to be tried there too, and they'll eat him for supper!" She added with a naughty twinkle.

I'd told them about Mac's revelations earlier, his invitation to become one of the Guardians. Once again I was so grateful to Amelia. Is there anything she can't do?

In a very quiet voice Jay asked, "Does anyone have any idea what we should say to the press?" I could see she was anxious as well. John had his arm round me, it made me feel better, Andrew did the same with Jay.

"We could announce our wedding? A double wedding, next week if possible. Well, some of us have to get back to Mars." Andrew smiled at Jay and kissed her cheek.

What a lovely surprise, and what an amazing idea. I was going all gooey and romantic.

"Andrew, aren't you forgetting something?" Jay was eyeing him enquiringly.

"Yes. OK by you James?"

"Andrew!" Jay was staring at him in disbelief.

Oh Andrew, I thought, surely not?

"Um, yes, well……. I should have asked you first." As he said this he did the one knee thing, wobbling exactly as John had. He held her hand, "Will you marry me, Jay? Here on Earth next week?"

"Yes, please," her simple reply.

And that is what happened on Tuesday the fourth of September.

It was a beautiful day. John begged me to wear my emerald green dress with the gold shoes and my new green hair clasp. Jay wanted to wear her red dress and we dashed over to the boutique and bought the lovely red hair slide I'd seen before. We also found Jay a pair of gorgeous gold shoes. The grown-ups thought we were mad not to want fancy wedding dresses and a big fuss but we were adamant.

There is so much tradition and ritual concerned with weddings. Ours was very simple. We did agree to Papa giving us away, one on each arm as he lead us into the marriage room. Otto was joint best man, standing beside each Andrew in turn. Such a happy occasion with another delicious meal at Umberto's afterwards, and far too much Champagne.

Amelia insisted on paying for our honeymoons for a wedding present and asked us where in the world we wanted to go.

"Arles!" John and I said together.

"Can we go there too?" Jay asked shyly. So we did, for two glorious weeks.

John and I are sitting on a rug in our romantic

meadow, surrounded by fields of sunflowers. He's watching the swallows and fiddling with my hair while I finish this, and the sun's going down making a fabulous Turneresque sky.

I needn't have worried about Papa and Otto. They were treated as heroes for exposing the Guardians appalling plans for termination on Earth. Their case was thrown out of court and they were back home again before October.

The Guardians faced impeachment and charges of genocide, MacKenzie beside them. They are spending the rest of their lives working in the mines on Titan, ironically their own worst form of punishment.

As for the press, we were what Papa called a nine day wonder. Especially after Henri pinned a large notice on the front door, saying "GO AWAY- BUY THE BOOK." They did too. It sold in it's millions.

About the Author

My career has been very mixed, from library assistant, laboratory technician to vehicle hire, which involved driving lorries around London, to finally using my technical skills as a couture dressmaker for many years, thus enabling me to work from home while my three children were young. I am a royalist, and although I've never met the Queen, many of my clothes have!

The one constant throughout everything has been my love of writing. I wrote my first story when I was six, called 'The Teddy Bear Who Never Got to the Moon!' I have no idea what became of it, I only remember my teacher being unimpressed because I'd turned my exercise book upside down and written in the back! In no uncertain terms I was told, it was for school work not for scribbling in! She didn't appreciate my attempts at illustration, either!

As a family we have lived all over the place. Starting life in North London, after 15 moves we are now back here, this time in the East, that is until itchy feet take over and we find somewhere else.

Printed in Great Britain
by Amazon